PLAYING WITH FIRE

MCKENZIE BROTHERS #3

LEXI BUCHANAN

HFCA Publishing House

Ireland

www.lexibuchanan.net

First Published 2013
This Edition 2024

Cover Design: Alison Chaffin Higson
Editor: Sirena Van Schaik
BETA Readers: Emma Clifton, Heidy Bendana, Kristy Louise Garbutt,
Nadine Winningham

SYNOPSIS

Sebastian had never been so drawn to a woman in his thirty-four years. Oh, he's felt instant lust more times than he cares to remember. However, something about Carla piques his interest, and he can't get her out of his head, which is where she should be given that she is dating his brother.

Carla has been pretending to date Ramon for a while now in order to dodge her abusive ex and keep Ramon's family off his back. They'd been friends for a few years, so it was only natural for them to help each other out, but she didn't expect to fall for Ramon's brother, Sebastian.

Catch up with the McKenzies as they welcome twins into their family.

PROLOGUE
MICHAEL AND LILY'S WEDDING

Sebastian

LILY LOOKED STUNNING AS SHE WALKED DOWN THE aisle toward my extremely nervous brother, Michael.

My brothers and I had spent most of the day teasing Michael, which probably didn't help his nerves.

A grin spread across my face as I watched the reception crowd. I thought back to earlier in the day when the four of us had teased Michael about Lily getting cold feet and running, his lips tight with frustration.

Michael had gone white and dropped rather abruptly onto the chair behind him. Lucien made for the exit before Michael could react to our teasing. Michael asked him where he was going. Laughter filled the room when Lucien replied, "To ask Lily to run off with me," and Michael's face changed from white to red.

Eventually, Mom appeared and hit us all on the back of the head like she used to when we were kids. Her calming presence put a stop to the teasing. Even though the five of us towered over her these days, Mom still had it in her to keep us all in order.

You only had to look at Lily and Michael to see how much she loved him. They were "it" for each other. With Lily being pregnant, that was a bonus. I was looking forward to being an uncle.

Spotting Lily alone for the first time that day, I walked over to her. "Hey, beautiful." She really was beautiful, with her hair swept up and pearls in her ears and around her neck.

"Sebastian, you look handsome," she replied, wrapping her arms around my waist, and giving me a quick hug.

Stepping back, she continues to look at me, her forehead creasing in concentration. I shift under her gaze and smooth the creases of my shirt. I'd taken my jacket off, leaving me in the white silk shirt Lily had instructed us all to wear. Not that I'm complaining. Without the jacket, the shirt shows off my abs, which I got from hard work on our company's job sites, McKenzie Holdings.

I narrow my eyes and stare back at Lily, hoping to break her concentrated gaze. "Are you eyeing me up?" I ask, grinning.

"Yep. I'm trying to decide who I need to introduce you to," she said, grinning as I scanned the crowd around us.

"No, you're not going to introduce me to..." I trail off, my gaze stopping on a woman across the way. "Her."

My breath catches in my chest as she emerges from the marquee — if you could call it emerging. She practically floats with grace and elegance. She's breathtaking! She's one of the most beautiful women I've ever seen, with a tall, slim build and full breasts that accentuate her hourglass figure. Her long, dark hair cascades down her back and over her shoulders in curls.

"Ah, Sebastian."

"Who's she here with?" I urgently ask. I need to know. "Lily, who is that bodacious babe with?"

I wince at my tone. I've never been so desperate to

meet someone, especially a woman who seems so committed.

Lily snickers. "Did you just call her a bodacious babe? How old are you? Seventeen!"

"Trust me, no horny seventeen-year-old boy would think of doing what I'm thinking of doing to her." I'm not going to say what I want to do to her in front of Lily. Michael would kill me if I said any of that to his wife.

"Bodacious!"

"Bill and Ted's," I reply, not really listening.

"What?"

"Never mind. You haven't said who she's with." As I talk, I fight the urge to walk over and pull her to me. Instead, I watch her cross the lawn in front of us.

"You need to keep your zipper up. She's here with Ramon."

Ice splashes through my veins as I look at Lily. Her eyes sparkle with mirth, but the curve of her lips makes me realize she's serious.

"How can she be with Ramon?" That wasn't possible.

Michael has come up behind us. "Well, I guess our brother is finally serious about someone, and Lucien needs to get his facts straight in the future." Michael wraps his arms around Lily.

I grind my teeth as I think about this new problem—one I never expected to have. "She can't be with him. Are you sure?"

"I'm sorry, but she is," Lily tells me, sympathy clear in her eyes as she tilts her head to the side.

Ramon's girlfriend is walking toward me, and all I can do is wait, frozen to the spot.

Carla

As I walk out of the marquee, I glance around the yard, looking for Ramon. Where did he disappear to? I sigh and give up the search.

My gaze falls on the bride, who is standing with her new husband and the same attractive man who had been standing with the groom during the ceremony. I assume he's Michael and Ramon's brother, but I'm not sure which one. I know he isn't Lucien because I met him when I arrived. So, he must be Ruben or Sebastian. I can't explain my sudden interest in him. No matter how hard I try, I can't keep my eyes off him.

Before I can look away, I feel myself being drawn toward him. He hasn't taken his eyes off me, which makes me nervous and sends tingles to places they shouldn't go, considering I'm with his brother.

When I'm a few feet away from Lily, Michael, and the attractive man, I force myself to look at Lily. "Hi, Lily. Do you know where Ramon is?"

"I haven't seen him in a while."

She looks to her husband, then back to me. The entire time, I can feel the guy's gaze burning right through me.

"Let me introduce you to Sebastian, Michael's brother. Sebastian, this is Carla."

I turn toward him and freeze. His dark eyes hold mine in some sort of trance, making it impossible to look away.

He leans forward and takes my hand in his. "Carla, it's a pleasure to meet you," he purrs, his voice melting my insides. "Are you really with Ramon?"

His question snaps me back to reality, and I take a small step back. What the hell am I doing, being drawn in by Ramon's brother? My life is complicated enough without Sebastian adding to it. "It's great to meet you, but I'd better find Ramon," I murmur, turning quickly on my heels and dashing away.

What am I doing? I chide myself, but I can't slow my pace as I flee from Sebastian and the feelings he evokes in me. I pray he doesn't follow me because I'm not sure I have the strength to resist throwing myself at him. He has turned me inside out.

Back inside the marquee, I grab a glass of champagne, quickly gulping it down before grabbing another. Toward the back left, I spot an empty table and make my way to it, hoping to hide there for a while. Maybe I'll even spot Ramon from my perch.

The ceremony was beautiful, and Lily looked stunning in her wedding gown. She really was a glowing bride. When Michael saw Lily walking down the aisle, I noticed unshed tears in his eyes.

I wanted someone to love me unconditionally one day. I want someone I can love with my entire being. I wanted someone who would look at me the way Michael always looked at Lily—*Sebastian.*

I shake his image from my head. It won't do me any good to keep thinking about him. Instead, I smile at the memory of being in the ranch house with Ramon when the wedding cake arrived, much to Michael's embarrassment. I spent about an hour trying to figure out why a wedding cake would embarrass the groom. The cake had four layers, and there were scarves made of confectioners' sugar around the base of each one. There was nothing embarrassing about it, and even Ramon wasn't sure why Michael was uncomfortable. I finally found out that there was something more to the cake, or rather, to the scarves. Lily snickered when she told me. Her only words were, "It was the scarves, and you should use your imagination."

My cheeks heat as I think of all the things I could do with a set of scarves. The heat intensifies as I imagine Sebastian as my accomplice.

"Carla, I've been looking for you. I'm just going to help Ruben finish getting his car sorted, and then we'll leave. Is that okay?" Ramon quickly asks, startling me and dissipating my fantasy with wisps of guilt.

"Yes, that's fine," I say to his retreating back.

The band hired for the occasion is very good and has certainly entertained the guests, young and old alike. They have now started playing slower, romantic songs for the more amorous guests.

Michael leads Lily onto the dance floor and takes her into his arms as the singer announces that it's the last dance of the evening. He starts singing "I Don't Want to Miss a Thing," the original version of which was sung by Aerosmith.

I smile and stand up to leave, practically walking into Sebastian. I look into his eyes, unable to look away. I'm frozen to the spot.

"Dance with me, Carla. I know you're with my brother. I don't like it, but I'll respect it. Please, just one dance."

Without waiting for a response, he steps close, places one hand on my hip, and caresses my face with the other.

I inhale, rubbing my cheek against his palm, and a shiver runs through my body. I need to leave quickly because I want to stay here with this man. However, I won't break my promise to Ramon. After everything he's done for me, I just can't let him down. He's counting on me.

1

FIVE MONTHS LATER

Carla

WHAT THE HELL IS WRONG WITH ME? I CURSE. HERE I am, hiding like a naughty child in the pantry and wishing I could disappear. Even better, I wish I hadn't agreed to come today, but then I would've upset Lily.

It isn't fair! I stomp my foot, turn around abruptly, and begin pacing back and forth, trying to remember why I came into the pantry in the first place. I take a deep, calming breath and lean against the pantry shelf. Get it together, Carla! You're here for Lily.

I've become friends with Lily and her friend Sylvia over the past five months. The last thing I want to do is let Lily down, especially since she's so emotional, partly due to her pregnancy hormones.

I've witnessed Lily have a few emotional outbursts, which have been amusing at times. I've watched Michael, Lucien, and occasionally Ramon trying to hug and comfort her. There was no way I could have missed today, even if I'd had warning that he was going to be here.

After all, it is Lily's baby shower. Pippa is holding the event at the McKenzie ranch. Baby showers are supposed to be for women, right? The men are supposed to do something else, pat Michael on the back, and congratulate him on knocking Lily up. But not the McKenzie men. Michael is standing guard over Lily while everyone else fusses around her, waiting for his brothers to arrive.

Thanks to Ramon, I have about ten minutes before they arrive, which is why I'm hiding in the pantry. To be honest, I'm not hiding from the McKenzie men in general, but from one in particular. Sebastian.

Ever since Lily and Michael's wedding, I haven't been able to stop thinking about him. When I think about him, I always end up feeling hot and bothered, longing for him so intensely that I don't know what to do.

Every other week, Ramon takes me to his parents' house for Sunday lunch so I can relax with his family. Except it isn't relaxing for me. It means that every two weeks, I must endure being close to Sebastian without touching him. He always keeps his distance, which I know is for the best. But that doesn't stop the flare of jealousy or the twinge of pain in my heart when he looks at me, his smile slipping, and he turns cold and aloof. A few times, I've excused myself and disappeared into the bathroom to pull myself together and dab at my eyes.

I've caught Lily watching me a couple of times, and I know she realizes there's something strange between Ramon and me. I'm just surprised she hasn't asked anything because it's unlike her to stay quiet.

I sigh and glance at the shelves, hoping for an answer or at least finding the item I'm looking for. Despite my feelings for Sebastian, I love Ramon. He is my best friend and has been for years. I met him when he was working on a McKenzie project in Canada. My brother met him and introduced him to me. The three of us hit it off right away. Despite knowing Ramon for years, I only recently met his family while preparing for Lily and Michael's wedding.

I was surprised when I first met Ramon's family because none of them knew who I was. When Ramon told them he'd known me for years, they all looked skeptical. I couldn't really blame them. I suspected he hadn't mentioned me to them before because of his connection to my brother, Noah. It would have been awkward, considering what I suspect.

Neither Ramon nor I know where my brother has gone. One minute, everything seemed to be going well, and the next, he just left Lexington without saying anything to Ramon or leaving me a message. I was still in Canada at the time, and he didn't come home or call to let me know he was okay.

I shudder at the thought. My life in Canada hadn't been great. I fled the country after an ex-boyfriend beat me up while I was looking for my brother. Two weeks later, I arrived in Lexington covered in bruises with stitches above my eyebrow. I'd hoped my brother was in Lexington to help me, but when I arrived at Ramon's, my brother was nowhere to be found.

Ramon took me in, and we came to a twelve-month agreement.

I would live with him for a year and pretend to be his girlfriend. I can't figure out why he needs a pretend girlfriend though. Noah and Ramon had shared enough women when they were together in Canada, so that couldn't be the problem.

Idly running my fingers over a can of peas, I pondered the relationship between Ramon and my brother. I know without a doubt that Ramon misses my brother. I sometimes wonder if there was something more between them because Ramon seems angrier that Noah disappeared than a concerned friend would be.

Noah is a whole other problem. He might not be around, but I worry about him daily. All I can do is hope he's okay because I refuse to think otherwise.

Ramon has been supportive, and it's clear that he's worried about Noah. He even hired a private investigator about eight months ago, but there hasn't been any trace of my brother yet.

Sighing, I look out the window to my right and see my reflection. I reach up and touch a dark curl that has come loose from the clips holding most of my hair on top of my head. I haven't bothered with makeup except for the pink lip gloss I've slathered on my plump lips. Ramon told me I look sultry. Whatever that means.

I slide my hand down the fine silk of my wrap dress. The dress caresses my curves, and my high heels make my legs look great. Unfortunately, I haven't dressed for Sebastian. Had I known he was going to be here, I would have worn more clothes. The first chance he gets, Sebastian will probably say something cutting about my appearance, which will send a dagger of pain straight through me.

With a heavy heart, I realize that I can't stay hidden in the pantry all day, but maybe I can get away with staying a few more minutes.

Sebastian

Why am I hesitating to attend Lily's baby shower? It's the hundredth time I've asked myself, but I know the answer—Carla. After one meeting at my brother's wedding, I couldn't forget her. Every time I close my eyes, I see her smiling at me the way she has over the past few months whenever she catches me at a weak moment. Other times, it's more like a scowl.

I can't blame her, really. I go out of my way to avoid her every time we meet, and when we're brought together, I hardly speak to her. I'm an idiot. I'm in my thirties, yet I'm acting like an embarrassed teenage boy with his first crush.

It really eats at me that she's with my brother. Regardless of whether she stays with Ramon—which isn't likely, given the way she reacts to me—I can't date her. When we were in our early twenties, we made a pact to never date a brother's ex. It's a pact we've kept all these years. Fuck.

Jumping down from the fence, I turned to make my way back to my parents' house, having detoured upon arrival to avoid going in.

When I climbed out of Ruben's truck, he and Ramon gave me strange looks, but whatever. We were supposed to meet Michael at his house after he got back from dropping Lily off at the ranch. However, my besotted brother decided to do things differently and insisted on staying with Lily.

As I trudge up the steps to the porch, my feet feel like lead. I don't want to go inside, but I know I must. I know that I'll seek her out and speak to her, which always takes a lot of my energy. I'm afraid that if I get to know her better, she'll get under my skin even more than she already has. I'm tired of staying away from her. In fact, I'm exhausted. Starting today, I'm going to talk to her like an adult instead of a lovesick fool.

I stumble on that thought. Hell no! There's no way in hell I can be in love with Carla. I don't do love like my sap of a brother. No way in hell.

After the baby shower, I'll hang out at Kenza and get laid. That's all I need—a release from the tension that's taken hold of me since I met her. I don't want a nameless fuck. I want my brother's woman. What kind of bastard does that make me?

How sick am I? It's been five months since I last had sex. I've tried, but every woman who threw herself at me just wasn't good enough. I always ended up at home, pumping my fist around my shaft as I thought about Carla playing dirty games. I break out in a sweat just thinking about it. I've lost count of how many times I've masturbated to the image of Carla, each time leaving me more frustrated than the last.

I can't figure out what's going on between Carla and my brother. She lives with Ramon, which doesn't sit well with me, given my obsession with her. But they never act like a couple in love—not like Michael and Lily.

As I reach the door, I run my hands over my face, a physical reminder that I'm putting a mask back on. As I run my hands through my already messy hair, I sigh with a heavy heart and brace myself to face Carla. Just as I'm about to push my way inside, the screen door flies open, narrowly missing hitting me. "What the hell?" I mutter, unsure if I'm cursing myself for being distracted or Ramon for rushing through the door.

"Sorry," Ramon grins, apologizing but looking anything but sorry.

"Yeah, right," I mutter under my breath as I push past him and enter the foyer of my parents' ranch house. It's the house I still consider home, even after living alone for ten or eleven years.

"Sebastian, you're here. I asked Ramon to go look for you." Lily walks toward me—or rather, waddles.

A quick glance at my brother causes the grin I've been trying to suppress to spread across my face. Michael is pussy-whipped, big time.

He's been on edge since Lily's belly started to expand, and this isn't the first time he's followed her around, hovering to make sure she's okay. Today is no exception. Michael looks like he's ready to blow a gasket with Lily wandering around, ignoring his suggestions.

When she reaches me, I pull her into my arms, holding her as close as possible despite the large belly between us, which she always displays with pride.

I smirk at Michael, who has come up behind Lily and started to rub her back.

"You look hot, Lily. There's something to be said about sexy pregnant women. But I'd better give you back to your husband before we end up fighting and get dumped in the horse trough." I kiss Lily on the forehead.

As I release her, Michael pulls her into his arms and smooths the hair behind one of her ears. Despite my teasing, Michael only has eyes for his wife and ignores my ribbing completely.

Just watching my brother with his wife sends an ache through my chest. Will I ever have what Michael has? I wonder, scanning the room. I know who I'm looking for, even though it pains me to think of it. Until I met Carla, I never considered having someone to call my own. I'm thirty-four and have never been in a relationship that lasted more than a couple of weeks. I've never been interested until now, but the woman I want is out of reach.

A slap on the back from my father brings me back to the present.

"I don't think a day went by without one of you getting dipped in the trough. Fond memories," Dad laughs, squeezing my shoulder.

"Yeah, and I seem to remember Sebastian ending up in there more than the rest of us," Ruben interrupts, walking up and wrapping his arm around my neck like a noose. He laughs as he does it.

I push him away and see Lily standing with her hands on her hips and her huge stomach sticking out. My eyes widen as I realize how ready Lily is to give birth.

"All this excitement is going to send me into labor! You do realize that, right?"

If I weren't so panicked by Lily's announcement, I would've laughed at everyone's shocked expressions, especially Michael's.

I rubbed my hands over my face and pointed behind Lily so she would turn and see Michael. He was standing behind her with a pale, pasty face, looking like he was about to pass out.

Lily reaches up, takes hold of his face, and pulls him down to meet her lips.

I turn away and meet my mom's eyes. She looks like she's holding back tears. I finally took off my jacket, held it in one hand, and pulled my mom in for a hug.

"Are you all right, Sebastian?" she asks softly against my chest. She keeps her arms around me.

I swallow the lump in my throat before answering, "I will be." I kiss the top of her head, then release her and move into the room.

"Go find Carla. She went to the pantry to get more lemonade." Mom gently nudges me toward the kitchen.

I shake my head and wonder if Mom knows how obsessed I am with Carla. I feel as though I've kept it hidden well enough, but then again, is it possible to keep anything from my mom? She used to frighten us when we were kids with all the things she knew.

In the small office, which is now an outdoor room for coats, boots, etc., I open the door, toss my jacket onto the rack, and miss. With an impatient sigh, I pick up the jacket from the floor and shove it onto a peg before turning toward the pantry.

Carla

THE SOUND OF THE DOOR OPENING BRINGS ME OUT OF my thoughts. Sebastian is standing there in all his masculine glory.

I really hadn't prepared myself for seeing him again. It's only been ten days since I last saw him, yet his presence overwhelms me.

After glancing behind him quickly, he steps into the pantry and closes the door, trapping us together.

My heart beats rapidly in my chest—it's a wonder he can't hear it. Unable to move, I stand by the room's one window and look through it. I don't see anything other than Sebastian's reflection in the glass as he comes to stand behind me.

I desperately want to lean into him and feel his body against my back. But I know that if I do, it will be even more difficult to stay away from him. I've always avoided anything that would bring us into skin-to-skin contact. Even when passing a dish or a drink to each other, we make sure our hands don't touch.

"Carla," he whispers. "Look at me."

Shaking my head, I reply, "No, I can't." My voice breaks as I bring my hand to my mouth. I feel close to tears with Sebastian standing behind me, mere inches separating us. I can always feel the heat coming from his body, beckoning me.

"Please, just turn around and look at me," he whispers, his voice pleading.

A tear escapes and trickles down my cheek. Hearing the man practically beg me to turn around and look at him is melting my insides.

Taking a deep breath, I turn to face the object of my desire. My eyes travel up his torso and linger on his whisker-covered jaw and sensual mouth before meeting his gaze.

I want to take a step forward and into his arms, but I force my feet to stay firmly in place.

"We can't stay in here," I croak, unable to get my vocal cords to work properly.

"Carla, what's going on with my brother?"

Sebastian reaches out, placing his palm against the side of my face in a soft caress and wiping away a lone tear with his thumb. I lean into his touch and hold his gaze as he lifts his other hand to my face and pulls me closer.

His touch makes me shiver. The shiver runs through me. If the slight shake of his hands is any indication, he's just as affected by our closeness.

Sebastian rests his forehead against mine, still cupping my face in his hands. He traces a line over my eyebrows, down my nose, and ends on my lips with his thumbs.

I need just one taste of him before I leave the pantry, the thought whispers through me as I swipe the tip of his thumb with my tongue.

He sucks in his breath, his eyes alight with passion.

Shit, I shouldn't have done that.

I pull away from him, make my way to the door,

stop, and turn around to look back at a stunned Sebastian. "I'm sorry. I can't be close to you because it hurts too much." I push through the door and let it close on him.

What have I done?

Not only is there an ache in my chest the size of Mount Everest, but there's also a throb between my thighs.

It's been well over twelve months since I've had sex—if you can call it that. It was a night of drunken pawing as my ex-boyfriend tried to maneuver out of his jeans and ended up falling off the bed into a heap on the floor. He hadn't even managed to get it up before passing out.

I knew then and there that we were over. It was a decision I'd gradually come to the week before his "little" incident. There had been no love lost between us. Until he showed up drunk and hit me, I thought he had forgotten all about me.

"Carla, are you all right?"

Lost in the past, I hadn't realized that I had walked back into the living room. "I'm fine, Pippa, just a bit distracted."

I smiled at the petite woman overseeing the shower. Sebastian's mom is delightful and deserves a medal for raising five difficult boys. I'd bet they're still difficult.

Pippa is intelligent, funny, and too shrewd for most people. She doesn't miss anything. Her eyes bore into me as she glances between Sebastian and me when he enters the room behind her. I try to ignore him and Pippa's look. A blush starts to work its way up my neck. I smile and nod toward Lily, who is being hugged fiercely by a friend who has just arrived.

I must flee before I make a foolish mistake, such as grabbing Sebastian's hand. He has moved to stand beside me with his mother on the other side. The heat from his body slowly seeps into my skin. My brain tells me to move away, but my heart and body tell me to grab his hand and never let go.

"Carla, come meet Sabrina. She's Lily's friend from England." Ramon takes my hand to lead me away. "I think she's opened Lucien's eyes," he smirks.

As he pulls me toward Lily and her friend, he leans in and wraps an arm around my waist. "Are you okay? You look pale."

"I wish everyone would stop asking me that. I'm fine. I'm just tired." I try to pull away slightly, but his arm tightens and prevents me from moving.

"Carla, I was wondering where you'd disappeared to," Lily says, pulling back from hugging Sabrina. Michael and Lucien stand like sentries in the background.

"I went to get more lemonade." It's still in the pantry, where Sebastian was distracting me.

Lily takes hold of Sabrina's arm and turns her around to face Ramon and me. "You've already met Ramon, so this is his girlfriend, Carla. Carla, this is Sabrina."

Ramon finally releases me so that I can hug Sabrina in greeting. "I've heard a lot about you and the antics the two of you used to get up to. It's good to finally put a face to the name," I say, pulling away.

Sabrina arrived back in the States about five months late due to the sudden death of her father. Lily had mentioned that Sabrina hadn't really gotten along with her father, but he was still her father. She missed him and had stayed to help her mother tie up loose ends.

They hadn't seen each other in person for eight years, although they had kept in touch via email and, more recently, live chat. Lily admits that she has missed her best friend, even though she has made many new friends.

"Oh, Sebastian," Lily says, looking directly behind me. Just then, I feel him slip his arm around my waist as he moves in and shakes Sabrina's hand.

What is he doing? I'm practically in his arms. My right breast pushes into his chest as he holds me tight. Surely, he can feel my aroused nipples through our clothes and know what he does to me. His arm around me feels like a vice, but also right. I reach out to steady myself by grabbing his arm, which brings me even closer.

"It's nice to meet you, Sabrina." Sebastian has his sexy grin plastered on his face, but I can see how tightly he's clenching his jaw. He wraps his fist in the back of my dress and pulls me closer before abruptly letting me go, turning, and walking straight out of the room, leaving me stunned.

I look around to see if anyone noticed what just happened between us. Everyone is busy talking except for Pippa, who's watching me from across the room with a thoughtful expression. It's anyone's guess what she's thinking, considering that I live with one of her sons but can't seem to stay away from another. She must have seen my reaction to him.

Sebastian

Fuck! How can she be dating my brother when she always reacts to me? I need to have my head examined. For now, though, a shot of whiskey would be nice.

"Sebastian, where are you sneaking off to?"

I turn and watch my dad walk toward me with a grin on his face. He looks good for sixty-four, without any of the middle-aged spread that my brothers and I used to tease him about.

"I need a drink," I reply, with my father standing in front of me. He always sees through my brothers and me, so I decide it's best not to meet his gaze. I also avoid running my fingers through my hair in a nervous gesture.

"Hmm, a bit early. Instead of a drink, go let George in." My dad points toward the porch just in time for us to watch George and Janet reach the door.

"Okay."

I hear laughter coming from the living room and

sigh with relief when my father leaves, leaving me to do his bidding.

I plaster a smile on my face and take the few short strides to the door to greet George. He's like family, and no matter how many times he's been told to just walk in, he refuses. That probably has more to do with him walking in on Michael and Lily and getting a look at more than he bargained for.

Chuckling, I open the door. "George, Janet...and Sylvia." I frown, looking for Sylvia's car. "No car?"

"It's in the garage, so Janet gave me a lift since she was coming from the city." Sylvia gives me a flirty smile and moves forward but stops abruptly and gives me a strange look. "Um, Sebastian, are you planning on letting us in?" Sylvia grins with her purple-stained lips. I'm still standing in the doorway like a brick wall. What the hell is wrong with me today?

"Sorry." I step back and follow them through to the living room. Yeah, I notice my brother Ramon's reaction when he spots Sylvia. What the fuck? My eyes widen in surprise. How can he look at Sylvia like that when he's with Carla?

I reach up and rub my temples because I can feel a tension headache coming on.

Not knowing what's going on with Ramon and

Carla is frustrating as hell, and I'm seconds away from grabbing Carla by the hand and declaring her mine.

Ramon can't keep his eyes off Sylvia, who does look different. Her blonde hair is swept up, with some loose bits around her face. But it's more her clothes. Apart from Lily and Michael's wedding, when she wore the revealing bridesmaid dress that nearly fell off her, her clothes aren't usually so revealing. Well, that isn't the case today. She has on a fitted dress that shows all her curves, the front dipping low between her breasts.

"Sebastian, please stop ogling the guests," Mom comments, slipping her arm around my waist.

"I'm not—" I pause mid-denial when my mom raises an eyebrow. "Okay, so I was. She looks different."

"More desirable?"

I decide it might be best to keep my mouth shut now that Mom's in matchmaking mode. The only woman I want to be matched with is Carla, but she's supposed to be with Ramon. After a quick glance in his direction, I see that he's still passing sly glances at Sylvia.

Unable to help myself, I glance at Carla, who's already watching me with my mom. She meets my heated gaze before turning back to Janet, who seems to be having a deep conversation with her.

"Perhaps you need to keep ogling Sylvia," Mom comments dryly, noting the direction of my gaze.

"I hear you, but I'm not having this conversation with you." I pull my mom close and kiss the top of her head. Then, I let her go and greet the new arrivals.

I wander over to Lucien, who is standing to the side, casting sly glances at Lily's friend, Sabrina. What the hell is up with my brothers today? "Not you as well," I grumble, stopping beside Lucien. Ruben comes up and shoves beers in our hands.

"Not you, what?" Lucien asks, taking a long pull on his beer.

"Sabrina," I say with glee, nodding in her direction. Lucien's eyes darken.

"She's hot...and have you seen the size of her—" Ruben trails off, seeing the look on Lucien's face.

"Don't finish that sentence," Lucien growls. I stiffen and search his gaze. He doesn't usually get so defensive with Ruben's teasing.

I know Ruben is only teasing, but it looks like our

brother is interested in Lily's friend. Oh, this should be good!

I turn to Ruben, wink, and say, "Since she's new in town, you should offer to show her around."

Mirth flashes in Ruben's eyes as he struggles to answer through his laughter when Lucien looks between the two of us. "Fuck you." With that, he follows Sabrina out of the room, leaving me whistling "Love Is in the Air" and Ruben laughing.

"That was fun," Ruben chuckles. But he stops when he catches sight of Carla walking past. "Carla, baby, come keep two bachelors' company," he says, wrapping his arm around her.

If I didn't know better, I'd say she looks uncomfortable. Ruben seems to pick up on it because he releases her.

"Carla, you and Ramon have been dating for a while now. Any sign of, well, you know?" Ruben asks, looking toward me for help. I stay silent, wanting to plant my fist in my brother's mouth.

Carla looks up at me, clears her throat, then looks back at Ruben. "Ah, no. Sorry, nothing like that."

Thank God!

Carla's eyes dart around as she looks everywhere

but at me. Anger slices through me, and I fight the urge to grab her and shake her until she looks at me. Yes, we're attracted to each other, but there's no need to ignore me. Fuck, who am I kidding? I've been ignoring her practically since we met at the wedding.

"Damn, I wouldn't mind having you as a sister-in-law. Besides, if he isn't interested, there are two more handsome McKenzie men right here." Ruben wraps his arm around my shoulders, a large, flirtatious grin spreading across his face.

Sometimes my brother and his mouth don't know when to stop. I push him away, trying to silence him for putting Carla in a difficult position. "What about Rosie?"

"What the hell are you talking about?" he scowls.

I quickly glance at Carla and notice a frown cross her features. I turn back to Ruben and watch his face darken with emotion. He turns and walks away, leaving me to watch his retreating back with a frown. I had no idea saying Rosie's name would cause such a reaction.

"Excuse him, Carla," I say as our eyes finally meet. "I'm not sure what's going on with him."

Carla smiles, brightening her whole face. "Don't

worry about it." She turns and watches Lily. "Don't they look good together?"

"Lucien and Sabrina?" I tease, having noticed that my brother didn't look so happy when he walked back into the room with Sabrina.

3

____

Carla

ATTENDING FAMILY GATHERINGS WITH RAMON ALWAYS stabs my heart. Part of me wishes my brother were here with me. In a way, it makes me feel homesick for my own family. Although Ramon's parents and siblings always make me feel welcome and treat me like one of them, I find it hard to accept while I still have no idea where Noah is, or if he's even alive.

As Ramon sits down beside me on the black leather sofa, I offer him a sad smile. He knows me well enough to know that I'm thinking about my brother. He leans into me and brushes my hair behind my ears, a friendly gesture. But my heart sinks when I see the look on Sebastian's face. He's sitting on the sofa to the left of Ramon and me. His features harden as he watches me with his brother.

"Carla, he'll be okay." Ramon wipes a tear from my cheek.

"How do you know that?" I whisper, hoping no one will overhear us. "You don't know where he is. Neither do I. He's out there alone. He might need help," my voice catching.

Ramon takes my hands and brings them up to his lips, kissing my knuckles. "He can take care of himself. You know that. He'll be in touch with us when he can."

I try to interrupt, but Ramon covers my mouth with his hand.

"Let me finish. I don't like the fact that he just disappeared. Yes, it bothers me. The private investigator I hired is still trying to find him." He pulls me into a hug, kisses my forehead, and sits back down on the sofa with me in his arms. "He'll be fine, Carla," he murmurs. I sigh into his comfort.

When I look into Sebastian's eyes, I see that they're full of questions, and maybe jealousy. Ramon and I have never been this intimate in front of his family before, so I'm surprised that no one else notices our exchange. Apart from Sylvia, who appears upset, no one else seems to notice. I've noticed that her eyes are always on Ramon when he's around, and I'm pretty sure he's aware of it. What a damn mess.

I try to move away from Ramon slightly, needing some breathing space, as Sabrina, Janet, and Sylvia take seats around the room with Pippa sitting beside Lily. Ruben and Lucien prop up one wall, and Elias stands in front of them, talking. Sebastian is still sitting on the sofa with George, shooting daggers at me with his eyes. He looks angry, too.

We did share an intimate moment in the pantry, and I would have liked to continue it if it weren't for Ramon and my promise to him.

Ramon squeezes my hand, bringing me back to the present, but not before I notice him looking between me and his brother. When he turns back toward me, he is frowning, but he tries to cover it up by kissing my lips. Then, he turns his attention to Lily and Michael.

Not knowing why Ramon suddenly decided to kiss me, especially after glancing at his brother, I chose to ignore them both for now and looked toward Lily, who was opening a gift from Janet and George.

When she finally opens the present, the first sign that it's not for the babies is Michael's flushed cheeks. He is hot under the collar.

Lily's whole face lights up as she takes the item by the hanger and holds the transparent negligee up for all to see.

All is quiet for a split second before Michael's brothers start whistling. A stern look from Pippa shuts them up.

"Oh my God," Janet says, jumping up from her seat by the window and running over to Lily with another gift in her hands. "Lily, I am so sorry. I was supposed to give you that one when the men left the room. The gift cards fell off in the car, so I had to guess, and I obviously guessed wrong."

"I'd say," Elias, Ramon's dad, mumbles, looking at his wife.

"Janet, it's fine. Please don't worry. I can't wait to try it on and show Michael." Lily grins and takes Michael's hand.

Once the chuckling dies down, Lily continues opening gifts for the twins, drawing lots of "oohs" and "ahhs" from Pippa. I can just imagine her being a hands-on grandma. She really is in her element with all the presents for her first grandbabies. Elias has teased that with Pippa around, no one else will get a look in with the babies.

If I were pregnant with twins, I think I would flip out completely. One baby would be enough to freak me out, let alone two.

Lily has quickly gotten through the gifts, and now all the wrapping has been cleared away, leaving the gifts laid out on the table. Janet clears her throat and says, "Well, I think it's time for the guys to leave."

I smile as Pippa asks, "Why do they have to leave? We still have all this food to enjoy?"

Janet winks at Pippa, but Sylvia answers, "Well, the other gifts we have for Lily might embarrass Michael, not to mention the gift-bearer and Lily."

A soft blush fills Pippa's cheeks as she finally realizes just how raunchy some of the gifts might be.

"Back in a minute," Ramon says, standing up and following his father and brothers out of the room. Elias turns back to Michael, pins him with his gaze, and says, "You stay where you are."

Before I have time to contemplate what's going on, the men return to the room carrying what look like two baby bassinets between them.

They position them in front of Lily and Michael, then remove the coverings. Everyone is stunned and silent, looking at the craftsmanship that went into making these. If I had to guess, I'd say Elias is responsible for them.

"Dad, did you—" Michael is unable to finish when his father nods. Michael moves to give his father a hug, then turns back to Lily and helps her up from the chair.

He brings her to his side and tries to wipe her tears away with the tissue Lucien gives him. Those two make me laugh sometimes with how they dote on Lily. If I didn't know better, I'd say she was in a relationship with both.

I'm not the only one watching the two men's antics. Sabrina sits beside Sylvia, frowning, probably wondering what on earth is going on.

Lily pulls away from Michael and turns to Lucien. He wraps her in his arms, then lets her go so she can hug her father and three brothers. Michael helps her get to her knees so she can get a closer look.

I watch and can't help but be in awe of the scene and the gift. The bassinets are beautiful, with what look like hand-carved pictures in the wood. Curiosity gets the better of me, so I stand and move closer. Crouching down, I start to trace some of the carvings with my finger.

When my finger slips over the image of a teddy bear, tears spring to my eyes. I read the inscription beside it: "To cuddle you close. Love, Uncle Sebastian." Oh my. I look up and meet Sebastian's eyes as a tear escapes.

Swiping at my face quickly with my fingers, I take a wobbly breath and look back at the bassinet. I move on to the next picture and inscription. A pair of boxing gloves. Really? I guess that they are from Ruben. Reading the inscription: "To defend you, Love Uncle Ruben," I see that I'm correct. I chuckle and move to the other side, where my fingers trace the ABC building blocks inscribed: "To build your dreams. Love, Uncle Ramon."

Emotions swell through me as I fight back tears. I'm so emotional today, and I hope I can hold it together until I'm alone, preferably back at the apartment or in Ramon's car. He's seen me cry often enough to handle me in tears, especially since I'm going to blame his family for their thoughtfulness in creating this amazing gift for Lily and Michael's babies.

My fingers trace two entwined hearts tied together with ribbon. The inscription reads: "You'll always have my heart. Love, your godfather, Uncle Lucien."

"Oh," I whisper to no one in particular.

"They're amazing, aren't they?" Janet says as I stand back up and notice the tears on her face. She points toward a large inscription inside the bassinet where I presume the baby's head will rest. As I look closer, I see a guardian angel with a prayer of protection underneath, followed by the words: "Mommy & Daddy."

I start to brush away the tears that I can no longer control. They fall even harder when Janet points out the poem on the foot: "Hush, little baby—" by "Love, Grandma and Grandpa."

Unexpectedly, Ramon extends his reassuring hand and places it on my shoulder. He passes me a tissue and embraces me. I stay in his arms, keeping my face hidden, until my tear ducts decide to have a dry spell.

A few minutes later, I pull away from Ramon and realize that I've soaked his shirt. "God, I'm sorry."

Ramon puts some distance between us and takes his shirt off. He then balls it up with one hand before pulling me in close to kiss my forehead. He chuckles. "Don't worry about it. You're not the only one to end up like a waterfall."

I keep my arm around Ramon and look around. There isn't a dry face in the room—and that includes the guys.

Everyone seems distracted by the gifts for the twins, except Sylvia, who keeps glancing at Ramon and me. Our arms are still wrapped around each other. Sebastian looks upset, but not because of the gifts.

"Are you okay now? I think it's the dirty presents now," Ramon whispers in my ear.

To anyone looking, we look like a loving couple. Little do they know.

"Yeah, I'll be fine." I flash him a grin, which he returns. He knows what I bought Lily.

He only knows because he caught me wrapping it the other night. Hiding it in the middle of the fruit bowl with yellow bananas wasn't the wisest choice, especially since the gift is fluorescent pink.

Sebastian

I snag a beer from the fridge on my way out back and take a long pull of the ice-cold drink before resting my arms on the porch railing. I gaze at the snow-capped mountains in the distance, but I don't see anything other than Carla wrapped around a shirtless Ramon.

What is happening today? First, she seemed ready to fall apart with just my touch in the pantry. Now, she's all over my brother.

Today is the first time I've seen them exchange more than a peck on the cheek, and I don't like it. In fact, I hate it. Way to go, Seb. Falling for your brother's woman.

"What's up your ass?" Ruben asks, leaning on the porch beside me but refusing to meet my gaze.

"Not in the mood for my brother's wisecracks today," I reply. "I could ask you the same."

He frowns and finally turns to look at me. When I get a good look at him in return, he doesn't look good.

"What's going on, brother? And don't give me shit. I know you, and there's something happening." After letting my words settle in, I add, "You're not getting enough sleep, and it's not because of a woman."

He stares at me while drinking his beer, then turns back to gaze at the unseen mountains.

"Fuck. This is for your ears only. You got me?" he says, glancing back at me quickly.

Starting off the way he has makes my stomach spasm. Ruben never has problems that he wants kept quiet.

"You got it." I put the bottle to my mouth and take a long drink while I wait for him to tell me what's going on.

"It's the club," he sighs. "Nothing financial. That's secure. Two nights ago, Keith caught a couple of guys trying to break into the club. They ran when they spotted him running toward them. But last night, more windows were broken."

"Fucking hell, again? Why your club? What the hell are they after in there?"

"Fuck if I know, but it's pissing me off. To top it all off, one of the waitresses is giving me a hard time. She ignores my requests and does whatever she thinks I mean. She spends most of her time bothering me. Why can't they just smile, keep their mouths shut, and serve the customers instead of bothering me so much?"

Thinking about what he just said makes me roar with laughter. He's upset about the vandalism and attempted break-in, but he was especially angry about the waitress. I'd bet my last dollar her name is Rosie.

"What's her name?" I keep the amusement out of my voice.

He takes his time answering. "Why? What difference does knowing her name make?"

He looks everywhere but at me when he says it, and I know I'm right even before he finishes speaking. "Her name wouldn't be Rosie, would it?" I chuckle at the look on his face. "You know what will get her out of your system?" Keeping a straight face during this conversation is hell.

"Do I even want to know what you're about to suggest?" Ruben glared at me while moving to sit on one of the chairs scattered around the porch.

I sit opposite him and grin. "Well, I was thinking naked, rope, and one or two of those toys you keep locked away." Yeah, my brother loves nothing more than being in control.

He's contemplating my suggestion—well, that's a first. Ruben loves his toys, but what guy doesn't?

"So, this is where you two disappeared to," Michael grumbles as he walks through the door and slumps into a chair on the porch. He looks exhausted. "Christ, I don't think I've ever been as stressed as I have been since meeting Lily. She's going to be the death of me."

Ramon laughs as he comes through the door, followed by Lucien, George, and my dad. He punches Michael's shoulder and teases, "She just might when you see what Carla bought her."

Michael and I look at Ramon, waiting for him to enlighten us. What on earth has she gotten Lily? I try to come up with something that I can imagine Carla buying, but nothing naughty comes to mind.

Ramon snickers. "All I'm going to say is that it's bright pink, and Carla tried to hide it in the fruit bowl with the bananas when I caught her about to wrap it in the kitchen." He starts laughing harder. "Oh God, it was the first thing I saw when I walked into the kitchen...fluorescent fucking pink." He finishes, shaking his head with a slight blush on his cheeks.

I wish he hadn't said anything while I try to count backwards in my head to regain control of my body. The thought of what Carla has obviously bought is making it difficult. I wonder if she likes to play and if she has any toys of her own.

"What's that grin on your face?" Lucien asks, kicking my foot from his position to the right of me. "Or should I ask who?"

"Thinking about something." I glance at him, meeting his knowing stare, and I know he's not going to let it go. I speak before he can start again, "So, what about Sabrina? She's pretty. Nice figure."

Lucien sits straighter in his chair and glares at me like a girl. "You stay away from her," he warns. "She's Lily's friend. Not someone you can sleep with and never see again."

"Lucien, calm down before your mother over-hears," Dad says, shutting him up. But it won't be the end of it.

It's kind of funny watching him squirm in his seat over a woman. He hasn't done that since the fire. In fact, this is the first time he's shown interest in anyone in a long time. Still, I'm not sure that going after Lily's friend is the best idea. As Lucien said, she isn't someone you can sleep with and never see again. Not that sleeping with her ever entered my head. The only woman I want was wrapped around Ramon not too long ago.

After a few minutes of silence, each of us lost in our own thoughts, I felt eyes on me. Looking up, I met Ramon's eyes. He was looking at me as though he was trying to see inside me. Have I given away my feelings for Carla? I refuse to call her his girlfriend. I'm so screwed.

"So, Sebastian, we're all curious about Jacky," Ramon says, still not breaking eye contact.

"What about Jacky?" Hearing her name alone makes my cock shrivel and quiver against my balls. She wants a McKenzie, and any one of us will do. But while she's my secretary, I can't escape.

I'll admit that, at first, her sexy body in tight clothes got to me. She has a set of tits to make a man's mouth water. Once or twice, I almost gave in to the temptation to put my cock between her thighs, especially when she bent over my conference table on purpose. But there is no way in hell I intend to follow through, especially since I've met Carla. I need a distraction because I can't carry on craving my brother's woman like I have for the past five months.

"She always looks like she left part of her clothes at home," says Ramon, which everyone seems to find funny except me. "I mean, she's mighty fine with one hell of a—" he trails off when Dad glares at him.

"Ramon, as I recall, you have a lovely girl inside with the ladies. You shouldn't be noticing the attributes of someone else." Dad frowns, watching Ramon's reaction to his comment. "You are serious about Carla, aren't you?"

Ramon lets out a sigh and rubs his brows as though he has a headache. "We're dating. We're also friends." Ramon glances at me before looking back at Dad. "She's living with me while she gets back on her feet. She insisted on doing my paperwork while Stephanie is on maternity leave, so she works in the home office. And, before you get the wrong idea, I pay her the same as I paid Stephanie, which was a real battle." He rubs his hands over his face as though exhausted, then meets my eyes. "So now you know why Carla lives with me."

What is he trying to tell me? There is no way I can mistake the direction of his statement. I haven't had that many beers, but if there's a meaning behind his words, it escapes me.

"We've gone off track here. I still want to hear about Sebastian and Jacky," Ruben interrupts, refusing to let me off the hook.

"There is no Sebastian and Jacky," I snap. "I have no interest in her, and this conversation is over." I stand up, toss my empty bottle into the barrel Dad keeps on the porch behind Mom's planters, and turn back to face my brothers, who are all smirking. Even George seems to be enjoying himself at my expense.

"Well, son, I can't say I know exactly what's going on, but I think you need to keep your zipper fastened around the staff."

While my brothers try to control their laughter, I just look at Dad, speechless. He always finds a way to make you feel like a teenager who's been caught in the hayloft with a gorgeous girl. "This zipper's stayed fastened for over five months." My eyes quickly go to my dad.

To add to my embarrassment, Lucien motions me to turn around. I do, and I come face-to-face with Carla.

Great!

4

Carla

WHO ARE THEY TELLING HIM TO KEEP HIS ZIPPER UP for? Relief washes over me when I hear Sebastian's words. Did he just admit to keeping his zipper up for five months? Is that because he met me? Am I the only one he wants? I try to hide the smile threatening to break out over that revelation. It shouldn't, and he certainly shouldn't feel that way toward me when he thinks I'm into his brother.

I clear my throat, gaze up at Sebastian, and say, "We're finished. If you want to come back inside, you can."

I turn around and start walking back toward the

living room, where everyone is still laughing with Lily at the presents she just received.

The men are in for a shock when they see the bounty set out on the table. Poor Michael. He's going to get teased by his brothers when they see the racier gifts—handcuffs, crotchless panties, a nipple care gift set, and a fluorescent pink "rampant rabbit" vibrator.

When Lily first opened it, I thought Pippa was about to have a heart attack when she realized what it was. Then she started laughing and said Michael would be frustrated until after the babies were born. For a split second, everyone went silent before we all started laughing uncontrollably. We tried to calm down before sending Lily into labor.

When I arrived back in the living room, I came to an abrupt stop when I spotted the "rabbit" slap-bang in the middle of the table, out of its box and looking ready to go. Oh my god! When I left the room, it had been on the side in its box. Now, there was no chance it would be missed.

I felt arms wrap around me from behind and realized it was either that or be knocked over. Well, that will teach me to stop suddenly. I feel a body press up against my back, and I smell his cologne. It's Sebastian holding onto me.

His breath was hot against my neck as he groaned into my ear. Needles of lust shot straight to my core as he pulled me closer. I turn my head to face him and watch as he removes his gaze from the pink object and meets mine. I want nothing more than to turn in his arms, seal our lips together, and press harder against his aroused body.

"Holy fuck."

Ruben's choice of words breaks the spell between us. Sebastian slowly starts to pull his hands away from me, leaving a trail of heat behind.

I take a few steps forward and practically wilt onto the sofa. My legs feel like Jell-O and can no longer hold me up.

"Ruben Elias McKenzie," Pippa shouts, making me jump. "You're not too old to have your mouth washed out with soap and water."

Looking bashful, Ruben replies, "Yes, ma'am. I wasn't expecting to see...well, you know." He waves his arms around in the direction of the table.

Michael finally finds his voice. "Can't wait to play."

He saunters over to Lily with a sexy grin, matching hers. I overhear him whispering words of love to his heavily pregnant wife, and I find myself longing for someone to do the same for me. I catch him eyeing the goods on the table, which makes me chuckle. They're going to have some fun once the babies arrive—in more ways than one.

Ramon's hand falls on my shoulder. I glance up at him standing beside my chair. He smiles reassuringly at me, and we watch his brothers walk over to the table for a closer look. Lucien shoots sly glances at Sabrina, who returns a nervous grin before coming to sit on the sofa beside me.

Over the past few months, I've watched Lucien mainly because of Lily's attachment to him. He really does treat her like a sister, sometimes coming across as an overbearing big brother, which can be amusing. I've also seen him when he thinks no one is watching, and he looks lonely. From what I've gathered from Ramon, Lucien hasn't had any female company since the car fire, which is sad because he has a lot to offer. Despite the scars on one side of his face and neck, he is a handsome man with a great physique and a loving heart, which his family sees all the time. Especially when he's around Lily.

Perhaps Sabrina just needs time to adjust to life here in Lexington. After all, she grew up in Virginia before moving to England with her parents.

"We'll leave soon," Ramon whispers in my ear. I'd

forgotten he was standing behind me, lost in thought, trying not to think about Sebastian and what it felt like to be in his arms, pressed against his chest as his cock grew hard against me. Argh! Don't go there.

Without looking at Ramon, I take one of his hands and squeeze. "Okay," I say.

I let go of his hand and watch him walk off toward Ruben. Then, I turn to Sabrina, who has been watching our exchange.

"How are you finding your way around Lexington?" I ask, hoping to draw her out a bit. From what I've heard Lily say about Sabrina, I never would have thought she'd be shy, but she is.

"I love Lexington. It's been about ten years since I was last here with my parents, and not much has changed, at least from what I remember. My father was here to purchase a horse he'd wanted for a while," she says, smiling at what must be a fond memory. "He was so determined to have this particular horse, Sultan. He was black as night and ruled the stables," she chuckles. "What about you? You're not from around here."

"No, I was born in Montana, but I lived in Canada for most of my life until I moved in with Ramon a while back."

Despite having my complete attention, I can feel Sebastian's eyes on me, begging me to turn and look at him. Why today? We've been together numerous times since we met, but it's never been like this with him—the heated looks and panty-wetting touches. Something's changed, and I'm not sure what.

"Carla?"

I blink and realize that Sabrina has been talking to me while I let Sebastian distract me again. "Sorry, what did you say?"

She smiles. "I asked you how you met Ramon, if it's not too personal a question."

I shake my head and reply, "No, it's fine. We met when Ramon was working on a McKenzie building project in Canada that my brother, Noah, was also working on. We all just hit it off. The rest, as they say, is history." I offer a small smile, hoping she hadn't noticed the catch in my voice when I said "Noah."

"At first, I thought you were with Sebastian. He can't take his eyes off you," she shrugs, "but I'm not that good at recognizing these things anyway."

My stomach drops. Does she really expect me to comment on what she just said? God, I hope not.

Sebastian

It isn't such a great idea to check out the items on the table, which have been given to Lily and, I suppose, Michael, especially with the bright pink thing in the middle of the table. In all my sexual experience, I can honestly say that I have never seen one in bright pink before. I wasn't shocked by the toy—I mean, I've used similar ones on willing partners in the past—but damn, bright pink!

I refrain from making a crude comment toward Ruben, who is really into "toys," which aren't just for fun. Standing here looking at the collection, though, all I can think about is having Carla naked and hand-cuffed to the headboard of my bed while I use straw-berry-flavored nipple gel on her breasts and a pink vibrator to bring her to orgasm before slipping inside her.

Reaching down, I discreetly adjust myself in my jeans. Lucien snickers beside me but I ignore him. I turn my back to him and the table and glance at

Michael, who's watching us. He's probably making sure we don't borrow anything he wants to play with.

Smirking, I walk over to them and ask, "How's my beautiful sister doing?" I lean over and kiss Lily on the cheek. I crouch down in front of her and look her in the eye. She's beautiful, even more so with her pregnancy in full bloom.

"I'm fine. Thank you, Sebastian. What about you? You seem distracted."

I quickly glance at Carla, then back at Lily, who looks as though she can see everything going on in my head.

"Don't worry about me. I'd say you have your hands full with my brother." I take her hand and keep it in mine as I rest it in her lap.

"Hey, brother, stop mauling my wife. Go get your own," Michael grumbles from beside Lily.

I wink at Lily and respond, "I already have my woman right here." I laugh and kiss Lily on the knuckles before releasing her hand. "I'd check Ruben's pockets before he leaves." I grin as Lily starts to laugh and places her hands on her belly.

"I'm sure our brother doesn't need to borrow Lily's things," Michael replies.

"Why on earth would one of your brothers want

to borrow anything of Lily's?" Mom asks, coming up behind Michael. She walks around the chair and wraps her arm around my waist.

I know now why they say boys never grow up. All I want to do is make this situation worse for my brother and watch him squirm under Mom's scrutiny, as we've done countless times before. But I hold my tongue and wait for him to come up with an answer.

Lily comes to his rescue, though. "They're referring to the handcuffs."

"Hmmm," Mom says, exhaling. "You boys think I'm unaware of the concept of sex. Not only have I given birth five times, but I've also read Fifty Shades of Grey." She winks at Lily, who looks ready to burst into laughter. Mom walks away to join Dad and George, who are deep in conversation by the window.

Spotting Carla chatting with Sabrina, I decide it's time to leave. I want my brother's girlfriend with a passion I've never felt before. Being around all those sex toys and having erotic images shoot through my head is frustrating the hell out of me.

I slip out of the living room and walk onto the porch, but then I remember that I brought a jacket with me. Turning around, I head back inside. I reach for the door handle and push it open to find Carla clutching her jacket. I walk in and close the door behind me.

"What is it with you and small rooms?" I say, trying to lighten the mood, although I'm not sure why I closed the door. "Are you leaving?"

Carla licks her lips before replying, "Yeah, Ramon has some work to do."

I nod and retrieve my jacket from the hook as Carla tries to slip past me.

"What about a goodbye hug?" I ask. This is nothing unusual. We always say goodbye. The only difference this time is that we're alone. Usually, we stand at the front door and hug everyone.

"Okay," she agrees, taking the step needed to stand directly in front of me.

I drop my jacket, take hold of her shoulders, and pull her flush against me. I feel her arms go around my waist. She sighs against me in my arms as I pull her even tighter into my embrace.

"Carla." I close my eyes, breathing in her scent and feeling thankful for these five minutes with her. I caress her back, feeling her quiver under my touch. Her hand starts to caress my back. Her touch has me rock hard, which I'm positive she can feel. With her hand caressing my ass, my cock jumps as I hear her moan. I catch my breath.

"Sebastian, why does this feel so good? Being in your arms. I never want to let go." Carla abruptly pulls away, picks her jacket from the floor, looks at my groin, and then turns away with a flush along her beautiful cheekbones. "I shouldn't have said that. I'm sorry, but I need to leave."

I reach out and take hold of her arm, preventing her from slipping away. "You didn't say anything I wasn't thinking. Don't be embarrassed, Carla. I'm not sure what we're going to do about this thing between us, but we can't just ignore it. Not anymore. Please, Carla. Let me talk to my brother. You can't be in love with him when we have whatever this is."

Pain fills her eyes, and her lips tighten as she fights the emotions overwhelming her. "We have to ignore it," she replies. Breaking free of my grasp, she gives me one last, heart-wrenching look before racing from the room.

What the fuck!

Without another thought, I grab my jacket and storm out the door, just missing Ramon. He looks surprised, but I ignore him and walk out onto the back porch to try to catch my breath. I rest my arms on the railing and breathe deeply as I hear the door open behind me.

"I'm not going to ask what that was about, but we're heading out, so I'll catch you later," Ramon says to my back.

I glance over my shoulder and meet his worried eyes. "Okay."

He doesn't move, though, and continues watching me. "Are you okay?"

"I will be."

5

Carla

RAMON HAS BEEN ACTING WEIRD EVER SINCE WE LEFT his parents' house. Usually, we talk or listen to music on the way home, but neither of those things happened tonight. If I didn't know better, I'd say he's sulking.

I have no idea why he's sulking because the day was good. I thoroughly enjoyed my time with the women when Lily opened her "naughty" presents, which the guys couldn't stop looking at. Ramon seemed to enjoy being with his family. But at the end, when we were leaving, he seemed in a funk, and he still hasn't snapped out of it now that we're home.

I can even hear him slamming around in the kitchen. There are loud thumps as he closes cupboards, bangs as he sets things down on the countertop, and crashes as he moves around the room. I wince with each noise, feeling a headache slowly build. Okay, enough is enough.

I walk out of my room and head toward the kitchen. I stand in the doorway and watch Ramon slam around the kitchen. It takes a few minutes before he sees me. He stops and stares at me, looking guilty.

"What happened, Ramon? You were fine at your parents' house. Have I done something?"

He looks away, avoiding eye contact, and turns his back to me, leaning against the counter. "What's going on between you and my brother?"

I'm stunned. I know I shouldn't be, but I am. That was the last thing I expected him to ask. "I don't know what to say." I take a seat at the breakfast bar to the side of me and rest my elbows on the countertop, burying my face in my hands.

Before I realize it, Ramon is standing in front of me, peeling my hands away from my face. As I look up at him, leaning over the breakfast bar toward me, he doesn't look angry. He looks...resigned.

"Carla, I'm not angry with you. I am with Seb, but not you. He thinks we're dating, and yet he wants you. I'm not sure how I'm supposed to feel about that."

He sighs and rubs the back of his neck in agitation. "Sebastian is my brother. If I thought he was looking at you as just another conquest, then I'd be furious, but he isn't. He says he hasn't been with anyone for five months—which was when he first met you—and I believe him." He grins. "You have my brother tied in knots. I was thinking about letting him know that we're just friends to put him out of his misery. But I think he needs to suffer a little more for poaching what he thinks is mine."

Unbelievable, I think to myself. There isn't any jealousy. It's just sibling rivalry. "You wouldn't hold me to my promise to act as your girlfriend? Why? You said you needed me to pretend for twelve months. Why the change of heart?"

I'm panicking at the thought of not being his "pretend" girlfriend anymore. Would he ask me to leave? Surely, he won't. He knows I have nowhere else to go.

"Carla, please calm down." His gaze searches my face and softens with reassurance. "No matter what happens with our agreement, this is your home for as long as you want it to be, okay? The only way you will leave is if you want to, not because I've asked you to. That will never happen." He pauses. "So, is there something between you and Sebastian?" He raises an eyebrow.

A heated blush fills my cheeks. For a moment, I consider lying to Ramon, but we've never lied to each other before. Finally, I say, "What he makes me feel frightens me. We haven't been intimate yet, but I'm afraid that if I keep seeing him, we will be. I don't know what to do about it."

I turn to face Ramon and stare into his eyes to show him that I'm committed to my promises. "I promised you I would see the twelve months out, but it's getting harder every time I see him. I know he's struggling as well, because you're his brother, and he feels like he's betraying you." I swipe at a loose tear as it runs down my cheek. Ramon follows it with his eyes.

"I'm sorry, Carla. I had no idea any of this would happen when I asked you to help me out," he says, taking the seat next to me and starting to rub my back in a soothing motion.

"Can I ask you a question and get an honest answer?" I watch him closely for his reaction as I sit up and secure my hair with a band at the back of my head. I could use a shower, too, but that will have to wait.

"I guess," he agrees with a sigh, watching me nervously.

"Why did you want me to act as your—"

I raise my hand to stop him.

"Girlfriend? At the time, I thought it was to explain why I was living with you, and to protect me if Gary showed up to finish what he started in Canada. But every now and again, I get the feeling there's something you're not telling me."

His hands slip from my back where they had been comforting me. Instead, they move to his neck. He uses both hands to rub it, a sign that he's uncomfortable.

"My parents." He lets out a heavy sigh, then laughs, and looks back at me. "Or rather, my mom. She wants all her sons to be married and supply her with grandbabies. She's been even worse since Michael and Lily got married. It's not that easy for me. My life isn't what my parents would want for me—or rather, my choice in life partner."

Life partner? Life partner? Is he admitting to what I've suspected all along?

How do I ask him? Because I think I need it spelled out to me.

"Um, Ramon," I begin, "Noah's gay." I blurt out to a stunned Ramon, who, after a minute, starts laughing. "Are you?" Well, that shuts him up.

"Fuck. Yeah," he whispers seriously. "You might as well know, I'm gay," Ramon chokes out. He leaves the kitchen and moves into the attached living room. He collapses onto the sofa.

After watching Ramon for a few minutes, I slip from the stool and walk over to him. I take the seat beside him. I rest my head on his shoulder, and he wraps his arm around me, pulling me into him.

Cuddling against his chest, I ask, "Why can't you tell them, Ramon? They're your family and they love you. It might take a little while, but they'll come around." I squeeze his waist reassuringly. "You may have to put up with your brothers being assess, but at the end of the day, you're from a close-knit family. Whatever happens with your announcement, every-thing will work out with them eventually. You must know that."

He kisses me on the head. "It isn't that easy. I'm a grown man, and I've been keeping it from them for years—since I was nineteen. For eleven years, I've been lying to my family."

I push myself up slightly from his chest to meet his eyes. "Ramon, you haven't really lied. All you've done is kept it to yourself. Wait a minute. I've seen you with Sylvia. Whenever she walks into a room, your whole body reacts. Don't try to deny it because I've seen you more than once."

Ramon pulls me back down to him before answering. "You're right. I'm not sure what's going on with her. I feel a connection with her, but it scares the shit out of me. I've never been in a relationship with a woman before, and I'm not sure if I'm capable of being in one. I've been with women—more than I care to admit—usually with another guy present," he says with a shaky laugh. "Shit, I can't believe I just admitted that to you."

"It was probably easier than you thought, considering I know what you and Noah used to do."

"Yeah, he told me he talked to you about everything, although he did say you had no idea, he was bisexual."

I chuckle into his chest. "I wasn't born yesterday. I can read between the lines. I spent more time wondering than I did knowing, though. I won't say anything to anyone, Ramon. That's your decision to make when you're ready."

"God, I'm not sure if I'll ever be ready for that."

"Ramon?"

With my head still on his chest, I look up to meet his gaze. "You're not one hundred percent gay, are you? You're just as bisexual as my brother, which may be easier for your brothers to accept."

He lets out a breath as he leans back on the sofa and runs his fingers through my ponytail.

Ramon is a hot guy, but I've only ever seen him as a brother. Oh, once or twice, before I realized his preferences, I might have given him more than a passing thought. But that didn't last long.

"Carla, I'm not sure what to do about Seb. Explaining that there's nothing between us might cause more problems than it solves, but I can also see how torn you both are." He runs his fingers through my hair. "I can see the questions in your eyes. I saw you leave the coat room a few minutes before Sebastian did. I followed him outside and watched him for a few minutes before opening the porch door to check if he was okay. He left without coming back inside, which he's never done before. You looked upset."

"Oh boy." I sit up, remove my shoes, and say, "Let's just see what happens over the next week or two before making any decisions about our so-called relationship, okay? Nothing is going to happen overnight."

"You're right."

I stand and glance down at him, smirking. "As usual." I smile. "I'm going to shower before climbing into bed and finishing the book I'm reading, so I'll see you in the morning."

Sebastian

Almost a week ago, I was in the small room my parents call the coat room with Carla, the woman who has become an obsession of mine. Carla, who is sleeping with my brother, is slowly killing me.

Sitting in my brother's CEO chair, I look out over the Lexington skyline and crave someone I can never really be with.

She occupies my every waking moment. I see her smile. I remember how she quivered against me when

I held her. I also remember the look of lust in her eyes the last time she looked at me before leaving me alone in the room.

Glancing down at my lap, I see that my dick is hard as fuck in my pants from thinking about Carla. This is nothing new, as every time I think about her, I end up with blue balls unless I masturbate. I reach down, rearrange my throbbing shaft, and turn back to the desk to deal with the problems on the construction site just outside of town. I wish Michael were here to deal with them.

I keep telling myself this is only temporary. I hate being in the office every day because I prefer being out on the job sites, but until everything settles down after Lily has the twins, I'm stuck here full-time.

"Sebastian?"

Ugh, Jacky. I hadn't heard the office door open. I really need to get my head back in the game.

"Is there a problem?" I tried to keep my eyes above her chest. She has a great figure, which my brothers love to talk about. Even though I'm preoccupied with Carla, I'm still human, and I'm still a hot-blooded guy.

She walks toward the desk and bends over to place some papers in front of me.

The sight of her breasts nearly popping out of her

clothes nearly causes my eyes to bulge out of my head. I quickly meet her eyes and realize that I have reacted exactly as she wanted.

"I just need you to sign here and here," she says, walking around to my side of the desk and leaning into me.

Unable to concentrate with her practically naked body practically touching mine, I start to read through the letters before signing them, without looking at her.

I pass them back to her and watch her smile as she saunters across the office with an extra sway in her step. If her dress were any shorter, she'd be showing her ass.

As she opens the door, Ruben walks in and stops to give her a once-over. "Looking good, Jacky. Hope my brother's looking after you." After glancing at me, he starts laughing and ushers Jacky the rest of the way through the door.

He whistles and turns back to me. "She's one mighty fine woman, and those tits," he says, licking his lips.

"Fuck, will you do something about her? You're more diplomatic than I am. Tell her we have a dress code or something."

Ruben roars with laughter. "You know, after the shitty morning I've had, I didn't think anything could cheer me up." He points his finger at me. "You, my brother, have."

I grunt and try to ignore him. "What happened this morning?"

He runs his fingers through his hair—a McKenzie habit—before letting out a tired sigh. "Someone broke into Kenza again last night. The bastards trashed the back storeroom, but left everything else alone. I can't decide if they're after something in particular. If they are, I haven't a clue what it is. Or if they just want to cause trouble."

I sigh and glance out the big windows, trying to gather my thoughts. Kenza has been having trouble for a while now, which is damn frustrating. If we could pinpoint where the trouble is coming from, we could stop it. But right now, we're blind.

"Tell me what you need." I sit back in my chair and watch my brother try to get his emotions under control. He has always found it difficult to accept help from anyone, but I know this is more serious than anything he's faced before. He has no choice but to accept help from his family.

"I hate this. Asking for help."

Before answering, I sit back and rest my right ankle on my left knee. "We're brothers, Ruben. If you can't ask your brother for help when you need it, then something's wrong."

"I know, and yeah, I'll call you when I need you there."

Hearing him agree tells me that this really is more serious, something he can't handle alone. I feel relieved that he accepted my help without much persuasion. I need to have this conversation with all my brothers to make sure everyone knows what's going on, because I bet he hasn't told anyone else.

"You need to get laid," Ruben informs me.

I look at him, startled by the abrupt change of subject. "How'd you get that out of 'calling me when you need me'? Are you serious?"

"You admitted to having a dry spell. You need to break it, and then you'll be chilled. I'm not sure I like you uptight. Besides, what about Jacky? She's yours for the taking."

I know what he's doing. I just wish he'd come up with a different subject. Yeah, I'm frustrated as hell, but Jacky? Hell no.

We both sit up straight in our chairs when we hear a knock on the door. Jacky comes strutting into the room in her black high heels, clutching more papers in her hand.

It's no wonder I never get much work done here with her coming and going every two minutes.

As she passes Ruben, I avoid eye contact with him but not before seeing him smirk with his eyes fixed on her ass.

He clears his throat, and we both look at him. "You know, Jacky," he quickly meets my eyes before looking away, "you should get Sebastian to bring you down to my club tonight. There's a live band, 'Deception.' They're good and going places."

I wince and glare at my traitorous brother as he stands up and quickly heads for the door. I grind my teeth together.

"See you both tonight," he says before closing the door on his way out.

If I take Jacky with me tonight, she'll get the wrong idea. How the hell do I get out of this mess my brother got me into?

While I was distracted, Jacky sat in the chair Ruben had just vacated. "It's okay, Sebastian. I know you're not interested in me, so don't worry about taking me anywhere. I know your brother dropped it on you."

She's crying. Why me? I stand up, walk around the desk, and crouch in front of her, offering her a tissue. "Jacky, you're a nice young woman." I pause. "It's just that I'm not really looking for a relationship right now."

Maybe if I start seeing someone, it'll take my mind off Carla, who I can never be with. I need to move on. But do I have it in me to move on right now? What the hell? "Jacky, you know what? Let's go to Kenza tonight and have a damn good time."

Her tears miraculously disappear. "You mean that? You're seriously going to take me out on a date?"

I stand and move to perch on the edge of my desk. "Yes," I whisper, wondering what the hell I'm doing. I need a distraction, but I'm not sure if Jacky is the kind of distraction I need or want.

Damn, Ruben!

6

Carla

GETTING THE SPREADSHEET DATA TOGETHER FOR Ramon is easier said than done when I can't stop thinking about Sebastian. I haven't seen him for almost a week, which is normal, but after the embrace we shared, I long to be in his arms tenfold more than usual. Just one look from him makes my heart flutter with excitement.

It was stupid of me to tell Ramon to leave things for a few weeks to see how everything goes. I could be with Sebastian right now, seeing where things go between us. I have a feeling that once I'm with Sebastian, he won't let me go. I've seen the possessive look on his face when he thinks no one is watching. Just knowing he's kept his zipper up since we met does things to my insides.

"Earth to Carla," Ramon says.

I press my hand against my chest in fright. "Where the hell did you come from?" I must have been so lost in my daydream about Sebastian that I hadn't heard the apartment door open.

"Sebastian," Ramon says, rubbing his temples. It was unnerving how easily Ramon could read my mind. "Look, I know you feel as though you owe me for helping you when you arrived in Lexington, but you don't. Noah is your brother, so I would have helped you anyway. In fact, I would have helped you regardless."

He crouches down beside me, and I spin slightly in my chair to face him. He takes my hands into his. His eyes are solemn as he rubs my hands with his fingers. "I asked you for twelve months to help me out." He shakes his head to stop me from interrupting. "But when I asked that of you, my brother wasn't in the equation. You hadn't even met him yet. You said you wanted to carry on as we are for a few weeks, but are you sure you still want to? Because I'll understand, and I'll even talk to Sebastian to smooth the way if that's what you want. You're a good person, Carla, and so is my brother."

I want to jump up and down and say, *"Yes, please talk to Sebastian and tell him our relationship isn't what he thinks it is,"* but something is holding me back. I think it's fear, but I can't be sure what I'm afraid of. Maybe it's fear of Sebastian rejecting me, though I don't think that will happen. But I can't shake it. Or maybe it's fear of the unknown, which makes my stomach churn.

"I'm scared, Ramon. What if he doesn't want me? Or what if he only wants one thing from me?"

"Then I'll beat the shit out of him."

I pull my hands free of Ramon's and glare at him while he laughs. When he realizes I'm serious, the laughter dies.

"Sorry, Carla, but are you serious? Yes, my brother wants to sleep with you," he cringes, "but he wants more than that. Sebastian has never gone too long without, and from what he's said, he hasn't been with anyone since he met you. That fact alone should tell you something. You won't know unless you give yourself a chance with him. I promise to beat the shit out of him if he doesn't treat you like a princess."

He makes me chuckle. "Princess, huh? I'm afraid I left my crown in Canada."

"Since you're such a smartass, I think I'm going to take you out to Kenza tonight. Ruben called and invited us. I initially told him we'd pass, but I think we could both use a night out. A night filled with distraction. So, what do you say?"

I nearly collided with him when I leapt from my chair, but he managed to rise to his feet. Before he could brace himself, I threw myself into his arms, kissed him on the cheek, and ran to the office door. I wanted to get a head start on pampering myself for tonight. It has been a long time since my last party, so I am going to indulge in a full-blown night out tonight. "How long do I have?" I asked Ramon over my shoulder as I reached the doorway.

"A couple of hours," he replies, getting comfortable in the chair I just vacated with his feet propped up on the desk.

Shaking my head, I leave him to it and dash to my room, where I stand in front of my closet, trying to decide what to wear.

Should I wear something sexy with my hair down, or should I wear a trouser suit that says hands-off?

I can't help but wonder if we'll bump into Sebastian. My teeth worry at my lips as I look at the selection. If he is there, I want to wear something sexy and sultry. Something that will make him want to touch me again. I know just the dress.

Smiling to myself, I open my closet doors and search the left side, where I keep my evening clothes. I find the slinky black dress I bought a while ago and have never worn. It should have cost five hundred dollars, but I bought it during a massive closing-down sale for seventy-five dollars. There was always the chance that they changed the original price tag to make the idiot—me—think I was getting a bargin. Nevertheless, I love this dress and look amazing in it. Ramon even did a double take when I tried it on for him. Since then, however, I haven't been able to work up the courage to wear it outside the apartment.

With giddy, almost nervous energy, I hang the dress on the closet door. I retrieve my strappy, four-inch sandals from the back of the closet and toss them onto the bed. Then, I walk into the bathroom for my primping session.

Sebastian

As I step out of the shower, I wince at my rigid dick. I'm tempted to look down and check if my balls have changed color because I'm extremely frustrated.

Trying to ignore the throbbing, I quickly scrub my body with the towel before throwing it in the laundry basket. I walk into the bedroom and yank on my clothes, starting with my pants.

Bastard! I can't zip them up. Quite frankly, I'll probably come within minutes given how aroused I am. Carla is under my skin and driving me crazy. I've lost count of how many times I've picked up the phone to call my brother and ask him to invite me over for dinner. I've even gotten into my car and found myself outside of Ramon's apartment building before coming to my senses.

My craving for Carla is an obsession that's overtaking my life, and I have no idea how to handle it. After holding her in my arms, I know she feels more for me than she should considering she's sleeping with my brother. It's like a punch in the gut every time I let my mind wander in that direction.

I take a deep breath, look down at my wayward body part, step back out of my trousers, and head back to the shower for some relief. There is no way in hell I want Jacky to think my cock wants to dip inside her.

Shuddering at that thought, I climb into the shower, turn on the water, and reach for the gel. I let the spray pound into the muscles on my back and coat my hand in gel before grabbing my weeping dick. I close my eyes and imagine Carla's smooth body running over mine as she presses herself against me. I smile as I squeeze my cock, imagining Carla raining kisses down my chest. The hot spray turns her delicate flesh pink, and her lips swell as she drops to her knees in front of me and licks the tip of my shaft. Groaning, I tip my head back and start to jerk off.

With my other hand, I massage my tight balls. Gripping the base of my cock, I continue jerking off as I imagine the feel of her warm lips sucking me into her mouth. As I stroke myself, I imagine Carla leaning against the low seat in the stand-up shower, her legs spread wide, beckoning to me. I position myself in her arms, her legs wrapping around my body as she pulls my cock deep inside her. I imagine how tight and wet her pussy is as I slide inside.

"Fuck! Fuck," I growl as I release, my jizz shooting

repeatedly onto the wall. I lock my knees before I end up on my ass.

What the hell is wrong with me? I'm a grown man acting like a kid who's just discovered the pleasure of masturbation.

I quickly dry off again, walk back into my bedroom, pick up my clothes, and pull them on. Well, at least my dick is behaving now.

My obsession with Carla is ridiculous, and I need to get over it. Tonight, I'm going to go out with Jacky and enjoy her company. I'm not interested in her as a long-term partner—not even for a night, to be totally honest—but she's there. Thanks to Ruben, the bastard, the date has been set. I owe him big time for what he did for me in the office earlier. There's no way I can let that slide. I'll get him back when he least expects it.

I fasten my Armani watch to my wrist, glance at it, and realize that I need to hurry if I'm going to pick up Jacky from her apartment on time and be a gentleman about it. Due to a family inheritance and vacancy at the right time, her apartment is three flights below mine. We don't often run into each other, which I was worried about initially.

After one last look in the mirror, I grab my keys,

lock up, and head to the stairwell. I walk down the stairs to Jacky's apartment. The entire way, I find myself hoping I won't mess up.

When I reach the door to her floor, I take a deep breath as I open the door and see her walking a hole in the carpet outside her apartment.

I stand and watch her while remaining unobserved. She's a beautiful woman with a slim body and magnificent breasts, as Ruben has informed me on more than one occasion. But she isn't Carla.

Dammit! Pushing away from the wall, I reveal my presence, causing Jacky to stop abruptly and look at me with nervous eyes. She seems unsure of how to react to me tonight.

Trying to put her at ease, I take her hand and kiss her knuckles. "Jacky, you look amazing." I flash her the panty-dropping grin a previous girlfriend said I had, and judging by her reaction, it's having some effect.

"You're not looking bad yourself, Sebastian." She looks me up and down.

Chill. I need to relax and enjoy her company. She's harmless. If I'm right, she's lonely and just wants company. Well, I can help her with that.

"Should we go? Ruben mentioned a live band," I

say, slipping my arm into the crook of hers and walking her to the elevator.

I hope Cody is waiting for us outside in the car. The last thing I need is small talk, especially since she looks uncomfortable in her shoes. And don't get me started on the dress—if you can call the bits of material barely covering the essentials that. Yeah, I keep trying to peek, but what the hell—I'm still a hot-blooded guy.

Carla

KENZA IS REALLY ROCKING WITH THE GROUP Deception on stage tonight. The lead singer, Phoenix, is a hottie, and so are Reece on the drums and Donovan on guitar. They're a well-put-together group, with talent and looks. Reece seems like a player. He kept giving me the eye before they took the stage. He also said a few sexy words to me when Ruben introduced us upon arrival.

Ramon keeps giving me funny looks and has been keeping me close. I think he expects some hunk to carry me off to his lair. Then again, he probably knows the only man I want to carry me off is Sebastian.

I sigh and take a swallow of the white wine Ramon has just shoved into my hand for the third time since I arrived.

"What's with the heavy sigh?" Ramon asks, wrapping his arms around me.

How did he hear me sigh with all this music going on?

"It doesn't matter," I shout into his ear, avoiding his gaze.

"Dammit! Um, Carla." Ramon looks behind me, then meets my eyes and pulls me tighter into his body.

I know exactly who's standing behind me without turning around, and I'm not sure I'm ready to be in the same space as him without throwing myself into his arms.

Ramon whispers in my ear. "I'm here for you. Turn around."

I turn around and my heart breaks when I see Jacky standing next to Sebastian. His arm is draped around her neck, and she's leaning into him playfully.

Emotions flood through me, and I'm not sure if I'm angry or disappointed. So much for wanting me.

At least I know where I stand before I make an even bigger fool of myself.

Ramon pulls me into his body and turns me toward the back of the club, where the seating is located. After pointing in the general direction for Sebastian to follow, Ramon starts leading us over to the group.

On the way to the club tonight, Ramon told me that he was going to talk to Sebastian about my ex, Gary. He said he was going to tell Sebastian that I'm living with Ramon only because of Gary and that we've been letting his family think we're an item for all these months. But it looks like that conversation doesn't need to take place now.

My legs feel like they won't hold me up anymore, so I gratefully sink into the sofa in the slightly quieter area, only to have Sebastian take up residence beside me. Why can't he sit with his date?

While I'm falling apart inside, trying to come up with an excuse to leave, he's sitting next to me, probably making faces at *her*.

Did Ramon know he was going to be here? Is that why he mentioned talking to Sebastian about our situation?

"Jacky, please dance with me," Ramon asks.

Traitor!

I glare his way, and he just laughs at my expression and walks off with Jacky, shaking his head.

I'm tense as I scan the crowd, debating how easily I can escape the table and leave Sebastian behind. Then he shifts, and all thoughts of fleeing disappear as he moves closer to me. "Ignoring me isn't going to work. You know that, right?"

I finally turn to meet his eyes, which is a huge mistake because I can't look away.

"Sebastian, please don't do this," I say, finally finding my voice. "You're here with Jacky, and I'm with Ramon. Let's just leave it."

Is he aware that those were some of the most difficult words I've ever uttered?

Over the past few months, I've really fallen for him. Seeing him with Jacky—who the brothers sometimes call the office shark—hurts. It hurts a lot. But what do you expect him to do, Carla? He's a grown man with urges, and he's gone five months without a woman, which looks as though it's about to change.

Feeling close to tears, I start to slip out from behind the table. But before I can make my escape, Sebastian is standing in front of me, looking angry.

"You keep telling me you're with my brother, yet

you always react to me. I've never seen you react to Ramon the way you do to me. But I can't wait around for you to decide who you want to be with. Imagining you in bed with Ramon drives me crazy," he says through clenched teeth as he reaches for me.

Stepping back, I try to collect my thoughts. "You're here with Jacky, Sebastian. You need to leave me alone. Maybe if you stop grabbing me every two minutes, you'll realize you don't want me after all and be able to continue with your parade of women."

I'm not sure if I'm warning him away or myself. I push away and dash for the restrooms, leaving Sebastian standing in frozen shock. I hope to hide in the restroom for a while, or even all night if Ramon lets me.

As I push through the crowd on the dance floor, I find myself with a pink feather boa wrapped around my neck. Then, as I remove it, a blonde woman with a Scottish accent—if I'm not mistaken—apologizes, "Sorry, lassie. My aim's a bit off. I had a wee bit too much to drink, I think," she says before hiccupping and wrapping herself around another blonde woman.

Well, at least some people are having fun. I think this as I continue pushing through the crowd of people still dancing and singing along to the band on stage. Ramon's presence causes me to smile, and I chuckle when I see Jacky rub her ass against his groin. My chuckling stops, though, when I see Sebastian pushing his way through the crowd toward us—or maybe toward me. This gets me moving again, seeking the escape the women's restroom will provide. I hope.

Only a couple of women are in the restroom, so I dive into an empty stall, pull the lid down, and sit while concentrating on breathing so the tears won't fall.

What am I doing? Damn Sebastian for bringing Jacky here with him tonight! Is he going to take her back to his place or stay at hers afterwards? If he had been alone, I would have let Ramon talk to him because my will to keep him away has weakened. I want Sebastian with all my heart, and I don't ever remember feeling jealous of anyone before.

"Carla? Are you in here?" Ramon shouts from the door.

"Maybe," I mumble in reply.

"What's going on?" He knocks on the stall door, and I picture him leaning against the wall with his arms crossed. "Carla, open the door and talk to me. Please."

Resigned to talking to Ramon, I slowly stand up, unlock the door, and walk out to meet his worried eyes. "Ramon, I'm okay. Just a bit—"

"Jealous," he finishes for me. "I'm not sure what's going on with him and Jacky, but the way he looked at you when you ran away tells me it's nothing. Jacky noticed as well." He grinned. "She wasn't impressed because he's supposed to be her date. He's dancing with her to calm her down."

My face must have shown my reaction to them dancing together because Ramon stands up straight, takes hold of my face, and turns me to face him. "Don't for one minute think my brother is going to sleep with her. He hasn't kept his mouth shut all this time just to sleep with her, regardless of what he said to you when you were alone together. We all know what Jacky's like, that she's looking for a husband with plenty of cash. Personally, I don't think she's too choosy."

The door to the bathroom opens, and I hear a sharp, "Okay, what the—" Ruben trails off.

I glance over Ramon's shoulder and see Sebastian watching me. Hurt reflects in his eyes. I wince at the image Ramon, and I are portraying—two lovers having a secret hookup in a restroom. God, this goes from bad to worse.

A muscle in Sebastian's jaw tightens. With one last withering glare, he turns on his heel and walks out of the restroom.

"Hey, bro," Ruben shouts after Sebastian. "Watch yourself. There's a bachelorette party back there."

Ruben turns back to us and stands in a fighter's stance, looking between the two of us.

"We received a complaint about someone making out in here. I had no idea it would be you two."

"We're not making out," Ramon tells his brother before looking back at me. "Will you be, okay?"

"Yeah, I think so."

Ramon steps back, putting me in Ruben's line of sight. When Ruben glances at me, his eyes widen. He looks back at Ramon and asks, "What's going on?"

Ramon runs his hands through his hair and looks at me. "Sebastian," he whispers.

Ruben starts to laugh. "You mean because he's here with Jacky?" Seeing Ramon nod, Ruben continues, "He's here with her because of me."

We both freeze upon hearing Ruben's words.

"Look, I was in the office earlier today while she

was there, so I told him to bring her to the club tonight before I could stop myself."

He slams his hand on the door to stop whoever is trying to enter from coming in. "Not now."

Leaning against the door, he looks back at us. "It appears I've screwed up, but I'm not sure how other than getting him out of his dry spell," he smirks.

Well, at least I know how he ended up here with Jacky. But what is he going to do about later?

Urgh! I've thought enough tonight. I either need to get drunk or leave. In my current mood, the latter is preferable. Otherwise, if I get drunk, I'll probably end up crying on Ramon's shoulder. Literally.

"Look, let's just leave and get out of here. Otherwise, Ruben's going to have a lot of unhappy customers," I say, pulling away from Ramon and walking out the door, with both guys following me.

"Rosie!" Ruben's roar frightens the life out of me. "What the fuck are you doing back here?"

Wow, there's clearly no love lost between those two. Looking more closely, though, Rosie looks upset.

"Um, boss," the bouncer from the door said, coming up behind us. "Someone grabbed her out on the floor. Sebastian got her free, but I think she's a bit shaken."

Ruben opens and closes his mouth, but nothing comes out. I spot a tear starting to trail down Rosie's face.

I push the men aside and walk over to her. "Rosie, will you let me help you?"

Seeing her nod, probably seconds before she melts down, I turn to Ruben. "Is there somewhere private I can take her?"

Without moving his eyes from Rosie, he points behind him.

Sebastian

What a mess. I blame my brother for this fuckup. With his damn mouth. Jacky gave me the perfect opportunity to say no, but I didn't want to be a jerk, and I wanted to stop thinking about Carla, so I agreed.

Now, she's off dancing with someone else, while I came to Rosie's rescue. While she was trying to free herself, some jerk grabbed her thigh and pulled her back against him. The asshole should be grateful that Ruben hadn't caught him, otherwise, he'd be in the ER. As it was, Keith, the bouncer, came and intervened, practically dragging the guy out of the club by his ear.

Ruben might not realize it yet, but he has an itch where Rosie is concerned.

Smiling, I turned to leave the dance floor, which looked to be taking a break. But I was accosted by a Scottish-sounding woman and her feather boa. "Hi, handsome," she said, shimmying her body around me. "We're looking for someone to strip for us because the dancer we'd booked for Emma's bachelorette party can't make it." She started making eyes at me while trying to put the feather boa around my neck. "You'd look good without your clothes."

Oh God, could tonight get any worse?

"Sorry—" Did she just squeeze my ass?

"Catherine, have you found anyone to replace—" a British woman says, stopping mid-sentence to take a good look at me. Little Miss Scottish—or rather, Catherine—rubs up against my ass, her hands moving slowly from my stomach down south.

Trying to stop her, I look up and see the other woman standing in front of me, licking her lips with a bright green feather boa. She moves in, practically falling against my chest.

"Um, ladies, I think you've both had a little too much to drink," I say, trying to untangle myself. I pray this whole act isn't being caught on camera and wonder where the fuck the bouncers are.

"I'm no lady. I'm Cat...you know, like Catwoman, because I'm good with a whip. You know what I'm saying?"

Oh, fuck!

Little Miss states, "I am Poison Ivy, and I would not object to sliding up and down your pole." Britain tries to bat her hands away from the buttons on my shirt that she's trying to slip open.

I hear a roar of laughter behind her and glance up to see my brother's eyes dancing with mirth behind Poison Ivy at my expense.

"You know what, ladies? Let me introduce you to my brother," I say, grinning at the look on Ruben's face when he catches on to what I'm up to.

"You mean there are two of you?" Poison Ivy mutters, spinning around and stumbling into Ruben. "Oh, wow, you're cute, big guy. Look at those muscles," she says, squeezing his arms. "Are you big all over?" she hiccups.

It's my turn to roar with laughter when I notice Carla talking to Rosie near the hallway leading to the restrooms and Ruben's office.

I need to talk to her and explain things about Jacky. I know she's with my brother, but I feel like a bastard for coming on to her one minute and going out on a date with someone else the next. Yeah, mixed signals, right?

"Ruben, I'll leave you to take care of your fan club." I look at Catwoman and Poison Ivy, grin, and then excuse myself. "Ladies, it's been a pleasure, but I have somewhere else to be. Ruben here will take real good care of you both. He likes whips."

As I walk toward Carla, I laugh at the expression on Ruben's face when I mention his liking of whips. I embellished the truth a bit because he likes his toys, but as far as I know, he's not into whips.

"Hey, Sebastian," Rosie says, looking sad until she sees my shirt, at which point a grin spreads across her face. "Um, pink suits you." She saunters off toward the bar.

Carla tries to slip past me, but I shoot my arm out to stop her. "Please, Carla. Let me talk to you. Let me explain."

She turns to look at me. It takes everything I have

not to reach out and pull her into my arms. Instead, I usher her back down the hallway and into Ruben's office for some privacy.

As I close the door, Carla sits on the edge of Ruben's desk, facing me. For once in my life, I can't think of anything to say.

She's wearing high heels that accentuate her already amazing legs. Leaning back against the door with my arms crossed, I lazily survey her body while unobserved by anyone but her. Earlier, I had noticed that the straps crisscrossing over her back held the slinky black dress over her breasts. The way the dress fits makes me wonder whether she has anything on underneath.

My breathing becomes uneven as lust takes hold of my body, hardening my cock.

Bringing her in here wasn't such a good idea.

8

Carla

Sebastian reminds me of a bull, ready to charge at the matador, breathing heavily with his nostrils flaring. The only difference is that the bull's eyes would be wide with anger, while Sebastian's are partly closed with lust.

I glance down his body and notice the bulge in his pants. I lick my lips. His cock twitches and the bulge grows larger.

"Fuck, Carla. Don't look at me like you're ready to suck me off," he says, closing his eyes.

I'm taken aback by his words, unable to comprehend him talking to me like that. I'm not a prude, and

I don't object to him speaking to me that way. In fact, it's a hell of a turn-on. I'm surprised that Sebastian said it when there hasn't been anything between us other than a hug and a few words, none of which involved sucking him off.

"You eye-fucked me. So what's your problem?" I counter, crossing my ankles and gripping Ruben's desk for dear life, because I'm seconds away from wrestling him to the floor.

He looks like he's fighting an internal demon, which probably involves both Ramon and me. What must it be like for him, wanting the woman he thinks is with his brother? It's all so messed up. I really wish Ramon were here to explain our relationship to Sebastian. Seeing him so tortured about it kills me, but since I don't know how much Ramon was going to tell Sebastian about our living arrangements, I stay silent.

"I didn't invite Jacky here tonight. My brother got me into this when he visited the office earlier today. I was going to tell her that I couldn't go on a date with her, but then she started crying, so here we are."

He looks gorgeous leaning against the door in his black pants and slightly unbuttoned white silk shirt.

There's just enough room for my tongue to slip in if we were lovers.

I've only seen him without a shirt once, at his parents' ranch, when he was playing football. My jaw practically dropped to the floor when I spotted him in boots and jeans. His chest was sculpted like a god's, with a six-pack that trailed down into a V. I'd seen it thanks to his jeans hanging low on his hips. Lily nudges me, bringing me out of my trance.

"Dare I ask what that look on your face is about?" he asks, watching me through heavily lidded eyes.

Without thinking of the consequences, I replied, "You." Then go on, "I was thinking about the time you played football at your parents' ranch wearing nothing but jeans and boots." I smiled. "Lily caught me drooling over you."

Now, he has a sexy grin on his face. "You were drooling over me," he says, slowly stalking toward me like a panther ready to pounce. "Do you have any idea how many times I've 'drooled' over you?" he grins. "Because it's too many times to count."

He uncrosses my ankles and slides his hands up my thighs, taking the hem of my dress with him, and steps between my widened thighs. His hands slide to my hips, which he squeezes before gripping my ass and pulling me into his aroused body.

I reach out and remove the pink and green feathers clinging to his shirt. I raise an eyebrow in question.

He laughs. "I got caught up in the middle of a bachelorette party out there and left them with Ruben to sort out."

I chuckle and start rubbing his arms, moving up toward his shoulders. Eventually, I'm able to slide my fingers through the hair at the nape of his neck— what I've wanted to do for a long time.

He flexes his hands on my hips, shivering when he feels my fingertips touch his skin. "I need to taste you," he says between clenched teeth as his cock throbs against my core.

When I move slightly, he hisses between his teeth as I rub against him. I wrap my legs around his.

"Fuck. Carla. Stop," he pants. "I'm seconds from ripping your panties off and fucking you on my brother's desk."

A groan escapes my lips before I can stop it. "I wouldn't complain."

I move my hands from his neck, wrap my arms around his waist, and drop my forehead to his chest.

Trying to regain control, I breathe in his scent, which makes me cling to him even harder. I want to burst into tears.

He gradually removes his hands from my ass, wrapping one arm around my back. His other hand holds my head to his chest, and he rests his chin on top of my head.

"I need to talk to Ramon because I'm falling for you, Carla. I've never felt this way about anyone before. Although it scares me, I can't ignore how you make me feel anymore. You're mine." He kisses my head and whispers, "Please don't sleep with him," into my hair.

"I promise to talk to him, but not tonight. Please. For me, Sebastian."

He nods while averting his eyes, but not before I see the hurt he's trying to hide.

Tears stream down my face as I realize this remarkable man is in pain because he believes I'm sleeping with his brother. I try to blink them away before he feels them through his shirt, but there are too many, and they continue to fall.

Sebastian stops caressing my back, uses his hand to cradle my chin, and lifts my tear-stained face to his. He uses his thumbs to try and stem the flow of tears. "Baby, please don't cry. Oh God, Carla."

"I don't sleep with him," I cry out just as the door opens. We both turn to see who interrupted us and find Ramon in the doorway.

He looks angry, but I'm not sure why. He knows about our attraction to each other and isn't concerned, so his anger doesn't make sense. I lightly push Sebastian's back before pulling away and walking toward Ramon. "Is everything all right?" I ask, placing my hand on his arm.

"It's fine, but we need to leave," he snaps, looking at his brother.

What the hell?

"Ramon, I don't understand—" I trail off when Jacky pushes past us, nearly knocking me over in her haste to reach Sebastian.

"Sebastian, I've been looking for you," she purrs, running her hands up his chest and around his neck, where mine were a few minutes ago.

I'm expecting Sebastian to push her away, so I'm surprised as hell when he puts his hands on her hips and smiles at her.

My stomach drops. "Get me out of here, Ramon," I say, as a startled Sebastian finally pushes Jacky away.

"Carla, wait," he calls as I run down the corridor. I hear Ramon telling him to leave it before I realize he's the one following me.

Sebastian

"Let her go. She's your brother's girl," Jacky tells me clutching my arm, either to keep me with her or to stop herself from face planting the floor, I'm not sure which.

God, one minute I'm telling Carla she's mine, and the next minute I'm clutching Jacky's hips and grinning at her. In my defense, I grabbed her so she wouldn't rub against me and feel my erection because knowing Jacky, she would have thought it was for her, and get the totally wrong idea.

"You know," Ruben says from the doorway, "I don't think I've ever had as much traffic or women in my office before tonight."

I laugh, releasing the tension that's had a hold of me since walking into the room with Carla. "You're only jealous brother." I grin. "What happened to the bachelorettes?"

"I owe you for that, *brother*," he says in warning, walking behind his desk. "If you're done for the night, I have work to do."

"I'll go, but we're straight." I glance to Jacky before glaring at Ruben, who laughs before getting back to his paperwork, shaking his head.

"What was that about?" Jacky ask, slurring her words.

"Nothing much. Let's go."

I take Jacky by the arm and lead her through the crowd in the club before finally getting outside to breathe in some fresh air. Jacky sways drunkenly on her heels and I glance at her warily hoping she doesn't get sick in the car.

Glancing at her she looks a bit green. "Are you going to make it home okay?"

Cody's just pulled up to the curb with the car. Jumping out, he looks at Jacky then me before hurrying to open the car door for her.

She practically falls into the car taking up most of the seat, but after some maneuvering I manage to sit as far away as possible in the town car. As Cody pulls away, she turns onto her side and curls up into the fetal position, giving me a view of her naked ass.

Closing my eyes, I rest my head along the back of the seat and try not to think about Jacky's naked pussy, which is wide open for my viewing pleasure with just one turn of my head.

It's been a long time since I had a woman's legs spread for me to sink my cock into, and the throbbing going on in my pants is only to be expected. But getting hard because of Jacky's naked pussy staring me in the face is making me feel guilty as hell.

Carla's getting her needs met by my brother so why the fuck can't I get mine met with someone else? And what the hell did she mean when she told me she didn't sleep with Ramon? They're dating and they live together.

Going round a corner, Jacky rolls onto her back with one leg going across my lap, her dress practically around her hips as her other leg drops to the floor.

Fuckin' bastard! I pull my eyes away, but they have a will of their own and keep going back to her pussy lips. Teasing me and my cock, which desperately wants to sink between her legs. Shit, not her legs, Carla's legs. What the fuck's wrong with me?

"Touch me," she whispers.

My eyes shoot to hers, which are heavily lidded as she's obviously been watching me lick my lips at the wetness I can see between her legs.

With slight hesitation, I tell her, "I can't."

Reaching for her dress with the intention of covering her up, she grabs one of my hands and puts it between her legs, coating my fingers with her arousal.

She moans and throws her head back as I dip my index finger inside her.

I can't do this. "Jacky, I'm sorry, but I can't give you what you want." As I pull back she scrambles to get upright and starts to lunge for me as Cody opens the door so I quickly climb out, nearly falling on my ass in my haste.

While trying to hide his laughter at my predicament, Cody offers his hand to help Jacky out of the car. "Would you like me to help you inside," he smirks.

Clearing my throat, I finally say, "No. I'll be fine." Praying I don't live to regret those words. "Have a good night, Cody"

She's my date for the night and, although it would

be easier to pass her on to him. I can't, in all consciousness, do that. I need to see her safely to her apartment door. And I mean door, so she better not pass the fuck out before getting up there.

Jacky is already clinging to my arm, so I wrap mine around hers and start walking toward our apartment building with her stumbling over her own feet as we reach the door.

"Wait," she mumbles, "I want to take my shoes off before I break my neck."

She leans into the wall to the side of us, and releasing my arm, bends down to remove her shoes. Standing she looks at me, smiles before grabbing my shirt and pulling me into her. Before I can get my brain into gear, she's practically climbed up me with her legs wrapping around my waist as she grinds against my traitorous cock.

Reaching out with my hands to support her, they land on her naked ass, which is when I realize her dress is up around her waist and her naked ass is on display for all to see.

"Jacky, stop. Please." I try to untangle her legs and arms, which have now gone around my neck.

"You're rock hard, you don't mean that," she whispers before slamming her mouth on mine when I open it to protest again.

It feels good having a warm and willing woman in my arms again. A woman that is grinding against my dick as though her life depends on it.

Hearing her groan, I come back to my senses and start thinking with the big brain, although right now it's a bit muddy as to which is the biggest.

Pulling away from her, I hold her at arm's length while she pushes her skirts back down to cover herself.

"You're hung up on your brother's girl," she wails in a voice that tells me she's about to cry.

Without answering, I usher her inside and straight into an elevator

I feel like the biggest dick around right now for not getting her off, but if I did that to ease my frustration, my guilt would be even worse, especially if Carla ever found out. We weren't exactly committed to each other, but I still consider her mine and expect her to think of me as hers and yet I've just been in a hell of a compromising position with Jacky.

Can my life get any more fucking complicated?

The elevator doors open with a drunken Jacky walking out who ignores me all the way to her apartment. I follow behind her wanting to make sure she actually gets inside, but there is no way in hell I'm going inside with her.

At her apartment door, she manages to get the door open before looking at me with such disgust written on her face then slams her door as I'm about to apologize, *again*.

What the fuck!

Women. Turning, I push through the door to the stairs and slowly walk back up to my empty apartment. My mind wanders away from Jacky and back to Carla and the 'I don't sleep with him' comment. It was strange, and I need to find the opportunity to ask her what she meant, otherwise it will drive me crazy.

Hearing my cell ring, I glance at the display before answering and see Ramon's name flashing.

"What's wrong?" It's unusual for one of my brothers to ring me so late at night, which puts me on alert.

"After the club, I drove to your apartment to talk to you."

Did he have Carla with him and why does he sound angry? "Then why didn't you come in?"

Oh god, no. I sag onto the sofa knowing what he's about to say.

"We didn't want to interrupt the show you were putting on."

We? "What do you mean we?" I ask, already knowing what he means.

"Carla was with me," he says. "I thought you should know."

9

Carla

Three days have passed since I last saw Sebastian, and I can't stop thinking about him. I should have been the one with my legs wrapped around him, not her. He broke my heart without even knowing it.

Talk about mixed signals! One minute he told me I was his and the next, he was practically having sex with his secretary for all to see.

As soon as I arrived home that night, Ramon tried to get me to talk to him, but I wouldn't give Sebastian the time of day. I just needed to escape to my room, knowing I was about to cry.

A couple of hours after I arrived home, though, I

received my first text from Sebastian. He said Jacky had taken him by surprise, and we obviously hadn't stayed long, otherwise we would have seen him push her away.

I didn't reply, and less than ten minutes later, he sent another text that made me crave his touch more than ever.

I slid my phone from my back pocket, scrolled through my messages, found the one from Sebastian, and read it again while wiping the tears from my eyes.

Carla, what's happening between us is real. What you saw tonight didn't go any further. She took me by surprise. Hopefully, the only woman I want is reading this message. I don't know exactly what's going on between you and my brother, but it needs to stop. You need to be with me. I want all of you—your mind, heart, and body. Thinking about your body makes me hard all the time, and I'm sick of using my hand while imagining what it would feel like to be between your thighs. I want to be with you. I want you to smile for me, and me alone. I want to look at you across the dinner table and know that we belong to each other. Don't give up on me before we can be an us. Please, Carla <3

I've never received such a sexy message before. I've read it so many times that I'm surprised the phone's scroll function still works.

I replied to him. How could I not, after the message he sent me? My message wasn't like his, but I replied anyway.

I love those words. If I'm being honest
with myself, I want those things. I
want you. Seeing you with her tonight
hurt, yet I believe what you said. I
want you, too, Sebastian. I just need
some space to work some things
out. <3

He has given me space. In fact, he hasn't replied or made an effort to contact me since. I should be relieved, but I'm not sure how to feel. Was he upset and angry because he sent me such a heartfelt message, only for me to reply and ask him for space? Have I totally messed up before things could even get started, like he asked me not to?

As I hear the apartment door open, I quickly wipe away my tears. But I'm not quick enough, and Ramon stops behind me.

"Carla, this really has to stop. You know that, right?" He turns me around, wraps his arms around me, and pulls me tight into his chest. "This is ridiculous. All this anguish between you and my brother could be resolved with just a few words."

Ramon is my best friend, and since I've been living with him, he's been like a brother to me, treating me like a sister most of the time. Right now, I need him to be my big brother in Noah's absence.

"We're going to talk," he whispers into my hair before pushing me away.

"We don't really need to. I'm fine."

He pushes me down onto the sofa. "Back in a minute. Don't move," he says, dashing into the kitchen.

I smile at Ramon's eagerness to pamper me, and I feel my tears drying up as I watch him brew coffee for us. For some reason, Ramon thinks he needs coffee to have a discussion with someone. Personally, I think it's so he has something to fidget with because he's rarely still.

"Here you go." He hands me my cup and sits beside me, propping his feet up on the coffee table like I am doing.

Ramon's apartment is large and spacious, with two huge sofas and two reclining chairs in the living area. I've fallen asleep on them more times than I care to admit.

I catch Ramon staring at me from the corner of my eye. I'm not sure I'm ready to discuss Sebastian, so I start a conversation that I know will freak him out. At least it will change the subject. "I think I'm being followed."

"What the fuck!" He quickly jumps to his feet,

slamming his drink down hard on the coffee table and spilling its contents, which he ignores. He turns fully toward me. "You think you're being followed? And you just decided to tell me now? What the hell is wrong with you, Carla? After what that bastard did to you? Fuck! You should have mentioned this sooner. Jesus Christ!" Ramon starts pacing back and forth in front of the window.

"Please sit with me," I say, tears running down my face.

"Fuck, Carla. God, don't do that."

He sits back down, pulls me into his arms, and settles back into the sofa. "Why didn't you tell me sooner? And don't think I haven't realized you changed the subject."

I chuckle into his chest. "I'm not too sure, really. Over the past couple of days, I've had the feeling that I'm being watched. I've looked around to see if I could spot anyone, but I haven't. Maybe I'm just imagining it."

"Do you really think it's all in your head? Seriously?" He asks this while stroking my hair, which lies freely down my back.

"Not really."

I knew Gary would find me eventually, and I

guess I should be surprised that he hasn't found me sooner. He can be terrifying and doesn't mind using his fists, as my body can attest to. But the thought of Ramon or one of his brothers getting hurt frightens me.

"I need to inform the building's security so he doesn't get inside, and you do not go anywhere unless someone is with you. You got me?"

My silence probably speaks volumes. I've never been good at doing as I'm told. In fact, I have a bad habit of doing the opposite.

"Carla, I'm serious. I need to talk to my brothers, tell them what's going on, and see if they can help out while I'm on site."

Inwardly, I groan. "I don't want anyone to get hurt because of me. What if he gets to Lily? We can't involve anyone else. Please, Ramon," I beg, giving him my *can't refuse me anything* eyes.

"That's not going to work this time. Have you forgotten what that bastard did to you last time, and what he threatened when you ran?"

He releases me, sits up, rests his elbows on his knees, and runs his hands through his hair. "We need help, Carla. I can't be with you twenty-four seven. I promise I'll only tell Sebastian, Lucien, and

Ruben, okay? I'll keep Michael out of it, and hope-fully, that will keep Lily away from it all. Shit! Sebastian isn't going to take this lightly," he says, looking at me.

"I know."

"Lucien called me on my way here to tell me to bring you to the folks' ranch for dinner. I'll talk to them alone and tell them what's going on. I'm also going to tell them that we're just friends."

I start to shake my head, but Ramon cuts me off. "He's my brother, Carla, and I've never seen him like this before. I can't let him continue to think you're mine. Admittedly, it was fun at first to see him want someone he thought he couldn't have. But I can't continue. Shit, my mom's going to be pissed."

"I can't go," I whisper. This brings his eyes back around to mine. "Everyone is going to be angry with me. Sebastian for not telling him the truth about us and your mom because she's always thinking about weddings and babies. Oh my God, Ramon. Please don't force me to go," I say in a childish whine, burying my face in my hands.

Ramon starts rubbing my back. "Look, the only person Sebastian is going to be mad at is me. In fact, my whole family is likely to be mad at me. I also don't want to leave you here alone, even though the security is some of the best in the city."

I can hear the wavering in his voice. Now, he's sitting, considering the pros and cons of my staying here.

"You really don't want to go?" he asks, rubbing his neck.

"I know I'll have to face everyone, but today, I really want to stay here. I'm going to read for a while to take my mind off everything, and then I'll shower and read some more." I smile at him and take his hand. "I'll be okay. I feel safe here, and I'm not sure I can handle Sebastian if he gets angry with me. Not today."

Ramon sighs, then leans in and kisses my cheek. "Okay, I'll let security know on the way out to not let anyone up to the apartment unless they check with me first."

"Thank you."

He kisses me again before standing up. "I'm going to take a quick shower first."

Without replying, I sit and watch him leave. I hope his family doesn't get too angry with him—or me, for that matter—because of our deception about our non-romantic relationship, especially Sebastian.

Sebastian

Ramon is starting to annoy me to no end by pacing back and forth while Lucien, Ruben, and I sit out on the back porch. Meanwhile, Dad is distracting Mom somewhere in the house.

On the drive to the ranch, I'd been looking forward to seeing Carla again, albeit feeling a bit nervous considering my text message to her the night of my near fall from grace. I was delighted with the first part of her reply but disappointed with the second part, more than I care to admit.

"Sebastian? You with me?"

I blink, bringing Ramon into focus. "Yeah." I rub the back of my neck as I watch my brother stare at me in surprise. "What did I miss?"

Lucien smirks, then shakes his head. Ruben starts to chuckle.

"Now that you've finished daydreaming, I have something serious to discuss with you all about Carla," Ramon says, looking directly at me when he says her name.

What is that supposed to mean?

"I promised her I wouldn't mention anything to Michael because she's afraid something might happen to Lily."

Lucien suddenly sits up from his lounging position in the chair. "What do you mean by that?" he asks. He sounds more serious than I've heard him in a long time. Then again, Ramon did mention Lily.

"Don't get your shorts in a wad, Lucien. This thing with Carla isn't going to affect anyone but her and maybe me."

"Dad will only be able to distract Mom for a little while, so save the macho stuff for later and tell us what you want to say," Ruben says, getting comfortable in the chair with his hands behind his head and his ankle crossed over his knee.

"When Carla arrived in Lexington, she was in bad shape. She'd been attacked."

"What the fuck?" I hiss, jumping to my feet.

Ramon puts his hand out to calm me down, but the fact that someone attacked my woman makes me see red.

I drop back into the chair and meet Ramon's eyes. I let him continue, trying to keep my temper under control, knowing the other two have questions after my outburst.

"Her ex beat her up looking for her brother, Noah. Noah was working on one of our sites here in Lexington, so as soon as Carla was released from the hospital, she came here looking for him. She was too scared to stay in Canada. What she didn't know was that I had no idea where her brother had disappeared to," Ramon says, frustration clear on his face. He looks away and then back at us. "One day, Noah was working construction, and the next, he was gone, and no one knows where. For Carla's sake, I hired a private detective to look for him, but there's been no luck so far."

"What happened to the ex?" Lucien asks. It's a valid question, and I'm thankful that at least one of us has a clear head.

"He disappeared before the police could arrest him, which brings me to why we're having this conversation."

With Ramon looking at me the way he is, blood starts to thunder in my ears. I just know I'm not going to like what he's about to say. It also clarifies whether he knows I have feelings for Carla. He wouldn't be talking to me directly otherwise.

"She told me earlier that she thinks she's being followed." I freeze as my brother continues, "She hasn't seen anyone, but I'm taking her seriously. If Carla says she's being followed, then I'm not taking any chances. I need everyone's help because she isn't going anywhere without one of us with her."

"She's not leaving my sight," I mutter to no one in particular.

"Um, Sebastian, don't you think you need to calm down a bit, considering it's Ramon's girl we're discussing here?"

Fuck. Ignoring Lucien and his comment, I turn to Ramon. "Where is she now? Who's with her?"

"She's stressed out and wanted to stay back at the apartment. She wasn't sure how everyone would react, and she couldn't handle anything else today."

"Is she alone?" I ask quietly.

He doesn't reply.

"I want to talk to you alone. Now."

I stand up and walk to the barn, with Ramon following behind me. Lucien and Ruben tried to come with us, but I overheard Ramon tell them that it was just between the two of us.

I smirk. He's damn right it's between the two of us. But what I really want is to hit something really hard—preferably Ramon's face—for leaving Carla alone when she was in trouble.

Hearing the door shut, I turn to face Ramon.

"I've never slept with Carla," he blurts out. I'm not sure I heard him right.

"What?"

"You heard me. We made up the relationship when she moved in with me, both to protect her and to keep Mom off my back about marriage and babies. Neither of us expected her to fall for you, or vice versa."

I slump down onto the workbench behind me upon hearing Ramon's revelation. "Why didn't she tell me?"

"At first because of her verbal agreement with me. Later, you'll have to ask her. As for leaving her alone in my apartment building, you know it has the best security around. Plus, the apartment is locked tight." I felt uneasy about leaving her, but I couldn't drag her with me when she was set on staying. She's like a sister to me, Sebastian. And I swear, brother or not, if you hurt her, you'll answer to me."

"I've no intention of hurting her." I start to pace, unsure of what he wants from me. "She's under my skin. No one has ever gotten under my skin before, and although it scares the shit out of me, I don't want to run from her. It's been killing me because I thought she was your girl."

Ramon laughs. "I know. It was fun at first, but after seeing how much it hurt Carla to keep you both apart, I told her I was going to talk to you about our agreement, but then this came up first."

"I'm going to her," I say, waiting for him to protest as I start to make for the door.

"Sebastian, don't hurt her," he says quietly.

I turn to look at him.

"I'll cut your dick off if you do," he threatens, and I fear he's only half joking. "I also won't be home tonight."

I grin as I walk to my car, but my grin soon vanishes when I think about the bastard who's after my woman.

10

Carla

As I step out of the shower, I hear my phone beep with a text message. I quickly dry my feet, wrap a towel around me, and dash to the living room to grab my phone.

Part of me hopes the message is from Sebastian, but deep down, I know it's from Ramon. After all, Sebastian hasn't messaged me since I asked for space.

I can't stop smiling when I look at the screen. It's Sebastian.

I'm outside the door. Don't want to frighten you. Please let me in.

I put my phone back down on the side table and dash to the door without thinking. After a quick look through the peephole, I unlock the door and catch my breath.

Sebastian is sexy in a business suit, but in jeans and a shirt, he takes my breath away.

He reaches out and places his hands on my hips. Without saying a word, he walks me back inside the apartment. Closing the door behind him with his foot, he turns and presses me up against the door.

He lifts his hand and locks the door again, then rests both his arms alongside my head without taking his eyes from mine.

Sebastian looks dangerous with his narrowed, lustful eyes. Being pinned against the door by his aroused body, coupled with that gaze, has my clit throbbing.

"I know you're not my brother's... all this time, Carla. We could have been together all this time." He rests his forehead against mine, our mouths mere inches apart. "I want you. I always envisioned that when I made love to you, it would be in a bed, nice and slow, so I could appreciate every inch of you," he whispers. "But slow will have to wait."

He kisses me in one of the most erotic ways I have

ever experienced, causing our tongues to entangle and our teeth to clash. His hands start to roam my body, igniting a fire within me that I never knew existed. I thread my fingers through his hair, holding his head in place while he yanks the towel from between us. He reaches for my ass and hoists me up against the door.

My legs wrap around his waist, and we continue kissing while he presses his swollen cock against me, sending needles of pleasure up my spine and to my nipples.

Using his hips and thighs, he keeps me pinned against the door while he removes his shirt and tosses it behind him. His eyes burn a path down my body as he takes in my naked form. My chest rises and falls with uneven breaths while his hands slide up from my waist to cup my breasts. His thumbs rub around my nipples. Before I can catch my breath, he bends down and sucks a nipple into his mouth. It sends a bolt of electricity straight to my pussy. I try to grind against him to ease the ache he's created, but I can't move because he has me pinned so tightly.

Sebastian growls, pulls me higher up the door, and slides a finger along my folds. "You're so wet," he says. He quickly unbuttons and unzips his jeans, taking hold of his fully engorged cock. Arousal leaks from the tip. His breath is hot against my skin as he whispers, "I need you now." The urgency in his voice matches the desire coursing through my veins, and I surrender completely to the passion he's ignited in me.

Supporting me with one powerful arm, he uses the other to grasp his rigid dick and guide himself toward me with a hunger identical to my own. He groans into my mouth as he slides deep inside me. I feel his warmth and strength enveloping me and know that this is where I belong.

I quiver around him, unable to stay still. Pleasure ripples down my spine as he moves within me. My breasts feel heavy and swollen, and my dusky pink nipples harden and rub against his chest. I arch my back, offering myself completely to him. He hisses and grips my hips tightly. "Don't move," he groans through gritted teeth.

I run my hands through the hair at the nape of his neck as he lifts his head and meets my gaze. "Condom."

"I'm safe. Birth control."

"I was tested four months ago. I haven't been with anyone since."

I smile at him. "Sebastian, stop talking and move."

The biggest grin I've ever seen splits his face. "Yes, ma'am."

Oh God!

The feel of his long cock sliding slowly out of me and back in just as slowly is causing delicious friction. I bite my bottom lip to stop myself from making whimpering noises, but one escapes just as our lips meet.

I wrap my arms tightly around his neck, and our tongues tangle as he starts thrusting into me so fast and hard that I wouldn't be surprised if he fucked me through the door.

With my orgasm fast approaching, I can't stop whimpering into Sebastian's mouth. He arches into me, pushing me down onto his hard shaft. He rotates his hips, grinding me on his cock and causing friction on my clit. Once. Twice. Then, I moan loudly, unable to contain the building pleasure any longer. Sebastian grips my hips firmly with his hands as he continues his relentless pace, driving me closer to the edge with each powerful thrust. My body tenses, and I shatter around him, crying out his name in ecstasy. He grunts in release and shoots his load deep inside me. I collapse against him, exhausted and breathless. With one last powerful jerk of his cock, he drops his forehead to my shoulder. I feel his warmth seep into my core and know that I belong to him completely.

"Fuck, Carla," Sebastian pants heavily into my neck.

He lifts his head and places a gentle kiss on my lips. "Please tell me you're my girl."

I brush the hair from his forehead, telling him what he wants to hear and what's in my heart, "I'm yours, Sebastian. I wanted to be yours from the moment we met. I fought against what you made me feel, but I'm yours now. You're mine. If that bitch, Jacky, touches you again, she'll lose a hand."

He grins at me. "Hold that thought." He lifts me from his semi-erect penis and helps me to my feet. "Are you okay if I let go for a minute?"

I chuckle. "Yeah, I think so."

He lets go of me, steps back, and pulls up his briefs and jeans, zipping them but leaving the button undone. Then, he looks at me—really looks at me—starting with the tip of my toes and gradually working his way up. He pauses around my hips and breasts, then meets my gaze again. His eyes are full of arousal.

"You're beautiful," he says, taking two steps toward me. "Tell me what you want."

There is only one answer to that question. "You."

Sebastian

"You," she whispered, a simple word that caused my heart to miss a beat. The small smile on her lips and the sparkle in her eyes, full of love for me, made it even more powerful. She loves me.

After taking her up against the door like a starving man, I carried her through to the bathroom and soaped her up in the shower. Just performing that simple task had made me hard as hell, ready to explode without her even putting her hands on me.

Needless to say, the minute we stepped out of the shower, I threw a towel at her to dry off while I did the same. I nearly shot my load all over the floor when I accidentally brushed against my erection with the towel.

We made it to the bed I'm now lying on, and

within seconds, I was in her. Both of us exploded in pleasure as soon as my cock slid inside her.

After waiting for over five months to have her naked in my arms, I couldn't bring myself to close my eyes. The thought of waking up and realizing that this amazing woman in my arms was a dream is terrifying. It would crush me to learn that I've been dreaming.

Smoothing my hand slowly down her back, I caress her hip and ass, unable to stop myself from touching her.

"Hmmm," she moans, slipping her leg between mine and pressing against me. I feel her hands on my ass, her nails scraping my skin, making my dick hard as steel. "You like that?" she whispers as I shudder in pleasure.

"I like anything that involves having your hands on me."

She snuggles further against my chest, and I tighten my arms around her, resting my chin on the top of her head.

"I'm sorry, Sebastian."

I freeze.

"I should have told you about Ramon and me. I promised him that I would go along with everything, but when he suggested talking to you about it, I told him to wait. My feelings for you make me nervous, and I wasn't sure how your parents would react to our deception. You know?"

It's frustrating knowing that we could have been together all this time. I've lost count of how many nights I've had to drink myself to sleep because I thought about Carla with my brother. Too many nights to count.

Carla pushes slightly out of my arms and lifts her head at my silence. "Sebastian," she says, her voice quivering.

I pull her back into my arms, roll her onto her back, and loom over her with my dick cradled between her thighs. I gaze into her eyes. "I'm not going to lie and tell you that it didn't bother me that you were with my brother because it did, a lot. But you're mine, Carla. Until you came along, I'd never wanted anyone to be mine. I hope you know how special that makes you."

She nods as I lean in and kiss her cherry-red lips, then her nose, before sealing my mouth over hers for a real taste. The minute our tongues meet, a charge of electricity shoots through me, nearly blowing the tip off my cock.

I press my hips down, grinding my cock between her pussy lips. She wraps her legs around my waist, and I continue sucking, chasing her tongue into her mouth. She's so wet, coating the length of me.

Our breathing becomes heavier as she breaks away from our kiss. "On your back."

I don't need to be told twice, and I take her with me as I roll onto my back again.

Carla takes hold of my face, slapping a sloppy kiss on my lips, and grins as she sits up on my stomach. She settles down on me, and my cock wedges between her ass cheeks, the tip poised at her entrance.

Gritting my teeth, I hold her hips still. "Do. Not. Move," I hiss.

Seeing her eyes fill with mischief should have warned me, but nothing could have prepared me for what happened next. She cupped her breasts and rubbed her nipples with her thumbs, throwing her head back as she started rocking on top of me.

"You're killing me." I thrust my hips up into her ass, my cock seeking its place between her legs.

I lift her up, holding her hips, while she reaches down, wraps her hand around my shaft, and guides me home. She slides down my length, enclosing me in her wet, tight heat. I let out a groan of pleasure.

"Fuck, don't squeeze me," I groan, trying to catch my breath, as she clenches her vaginal muscles and sucks me in deeper. Balls fucking deep.

"I have to."

When I release my grip on her hips, she slowly withdraws to the tip, squeezing and releasing, squeezing and releasing. "I have a confession to make," she whispered.

My hands freeze, stopping the circular motion I was making on her plump nipples.

"Over the past five months, I've fallen irrevocably in love with you."

I'd hoped she loved me because I love her, but hearing her say it leaves me speechless.

"Carla," I groan as she slams back down on me.

I hold her tightly, sit up, and wrap my arms around her as she wraps her arms around my neck. She stays kneeling over me with my cock buried deep inside her.

"I love you, too, you know," I say, placing light kisses along her lips, nose, eyes, and cheeks. Finally, I seal our lips together. I suck her tongue into my mouth and taste her. As I chase her tongue back into her mouth, she slowly starts to grind on me.

Having the woman I love wrapped around me as she makes love to me is the most erotic dance of my life. Knowing she loves me makes it ten times more pleasurable. She's mine now, and I'll fight anyone who tries to hurt her. I will move heaven and earth to keep her safe.

"Seb. Oh, God," she moans, breaking from our kiss and throwing her head back.

"Slow, baby." I kiss her neck, push her back slightly, and clamp my mouth down on one of her breasts as I thrust into her.

She's close, and I'm barely holding on. I start to feel tiny flutters up and down my cock. "Come for me, Carla. I can't hold on anymore."

Groaning, she comes apart, flooding my dick and groin with her wetness. I hold her against me, take one final thrust, and start shooting my release inside her. I experience a never-ending stream of pleasure.

Coming to our senses, Carla panted on my shoulder, her arms still wrapped around me. I breathed in her scent, my face buried in her neck. Not wanting to separate from her, yet knowing I need to clean us both up, I lie back on the bed and roll over with her so that her back is on the bed.

"I have no words for what I just experienced with you," I tell her, smiling broadly.

I place a quick kiss on her lips and start to pull out, but she has other ideas. She clamps down on my erect penis and wraps her legs around me.

She purred, reaching up to run her hands through my hair and pull me down to her lips. "Make love to me again." My hips press down, my dick is ready and eager for another round.

11

Carla

I STRETCHED MY BODY LIKE A CAT, ENJOYING EVERY aching muscle and sighing. It's definitely a perfect morning for a lazy day in bed, but I need to catch up on mundane tasks, such as laundry.

I have no desire to get out of bed or move beyond this initial stretch. I smiled, remembering the first night of passion with Sebastian. It was more than I could have ever dreamed of. Each day after that was even better. Every morning, when I woke up early, Sebastian was hard as steel inside me, which made my body relaxed and sated. He brought me to climax three times before taking his own pleasure. Unfortunately, he had to go to the office for a meeting that he couldn't get out of or postpone, unlike the past three days. Three days of pure bliss!

Seeing that Sebastian was planning on spending his time with me at the apartment, which has excellent security, Ramon had decided to go ahead with a business trip to New York and wouldn't be back until later today.

After stretching, I threw the quilt off and headed for the bathroom. I finished my morning routine in ten minutes, slid my legs into my black yoga pants and pink T-shirt, and put on my sneakers.

Feeling happy and relaxed, and looking forward to my day, I walked through to the kitchen for my second coffee, the first having been brought to me in bed while Sebastian kissed me goodbye, nearly causing him to climb back into bed with me.

Smiling to myself, I took a sip of my coffee and placed it on the breakfast bar to get something to eat. I reach below and grab the box of Fruit Loops, which Sebastian teases me about. It didn't stop him from eating two bowls yesterday morning.

I pour some into a bowl I retrieved from the dishwasher and pour milk on it. Sitting down to eat, I spot my phone, which is flashing with messages.

Unlocking my phone, I see that they are all from Sebastian except for one from Lily. Deciding that Lily's message is probably short and sweet, I read hers first.

> Carla, if you're free, do you want to have lunch at my house?

That is one question I can answer without even having to think about it.

> I'd love to! See you in an hour or so.

I continued munching on the Fruit Loops while starting to read through Sebastian's messages.

> I'm at work and missing you.

> I wish you were with me.

> When I left, I just wanted to climb back into bed with you. You have no idea how hard it was for me to leave.

I snicker.

> Carla, talk to me.

> Are you asleep?

> Carla, you're frustrating the hell out of me.

> Damn it, woman.

Deciding to put him out of his misery, I come up with a reply.

> I'm awake now. I woke up naked, wet, and hungry for you and the hardness between your legs.

I click send and smile. I know exactly what it will do to him, and I'm eager to think of another sexy message. After finishing the dishes, I collect my coffee and relax in the chair by the window, looking out at the skyline while typing another message.

> I'm thinking about last night when you let me suck you off. I'm thinking about how it felt to suck your balls into my mouth. Most of all, I'm thinking about how it felt, knowing my wet mouth can make you quiver and lose control so quickly.

Okay, maybe I shouldn't be so naughty. After all, he's at the office, possibly in a meeting, or worse, giving work instructions to Jacky. He'd promised to transfer her to another department if she continued touching him and trying to get into his pants.

Beep. Beep. Beep.

I can't keep the grin off my face when I unlock my phone and find his reply waiting for me.

> You are one wicked woman. My cock is hard as fuck, wanting inside your tight, wet cunt.

I'm startled by the "c" word at the end of Sebastian's message. Don't get me wrong, I'm not a prude. But Seb hasn't used that word before, and I can't decide whether I like it. My body certainly reacts to hearing it. I wonder how Sebastian's body will react to my next message if I use the "c" word?

> My cunt needs your cock.

I blush after clicking send. I've never spoken like that before, but before I can feel embarrassed, my phone rings.

Sebastian.

Still blushing, I answer.

"Hey, how are you doing?"

After a pause, he replies, "Is that a serious question, baby? Because after that last message, I'm so close to locking myself in the bathroom and having phone sex with you."

Oh God!

"Baby, I'm just kidding. I have a meeting about to start, but my cock is hard and throbbing, wanting to sink into that tight cunt of yours." He starts to chuckle when he says the "c" word out loud, making me gasp. "Carla, there's nothing wrong with dirty talk between lovers. When I get my hands on you, I'm going to whisper a hell of a lot more while I fuck you and make you come."

"Seb," I moan.

Before we got together three days ago, he'd get me wet. Now, he has me soaked!

"I love how you call me Seb. My brothers call me that on occasion, but I love hearing it on your lips," he tells me. I can hear someone talking in the background before Sebastian says, "I'll be right there." "Carla, I'm sorry. I have to go, but I promise to be back as soon as I can."

"Okay, but I'm heading over to Lily and Michael's place soon. Lily invited me to lunch, and before you say anything, I'll get security to escort me to my car. Then, I'll go straight there and straight back with no stops in between." I bite my lip, knowing he isn't going to like this.

"Promise me. You'll call security when you approach the building, and they'll meet you in the parking lot."

I can imagine Sebastian running his hands through his hair in frustration because he can't be with me when I leave the apartment.

"I promise. Now, go to your meeting, and don't worry about me."

"I love you, Carla. Always. I'll see you later."

"I love you, too."

I hung up and sat looking out the window for a few minutes, lost in thought. I wondered when Gary was going to show his violent side again.

Sebastian

The meeting finally ends, and I almost cheer as I watch everyone leave the office and head to the elevators. I walk back to my office and find Jacky bent over my desk, wiggling her butt.

"Jacky?" I shout, startling her, though I'm not sure she didn't hear me walk in behind her. It's my own damn fault she keeps throwing herself at me and my brothers.

As I move to stand behind my desk, I notice a freshly brewed coffee sitting there. I unload the documents from my arms while trying to think of something to say to get her to stop. If she weren't such a good worker, I'd have transferred her by now. The fact is, she's damn good at her job and keeps me organized.

"Look," I say, rubbing the back of my neck in discomfort. "Can we just have a working relationship here, Jacky? I'm with someone now, and I have no intention of letting her go."

I sit down, lean back, and offer her the seat opposite me. "You're an attractive woman, and there are lots of guys out there who would love to be with you—"

"But not you," she interrupted, crossing her arms and glaring at me.

"I'm sorry Jacky." Pause. "The woman I'm with means a lot to me, so you and I need to return to a professional relationship. I only took you out once, and nothing happened. So, um, do you think we can get along? Can you please stop, you know, doing that?" I wave my hands around.

She starts to laugh. "Are you asking me to stop flashing my ass and boobs in your face, and stop bending over things, which gives you ideas?"

"Yes, but no, fuck. I mean, yes, stop flashing your body in front of me, but no, you don't give me ideas." I let out a frustrated sigh. This woman is enough to drive a man to drink!

"I guess I can do that. If you're sure there isn't any chance with you." She sounds hopeful.

I shook my head and started flitting through the papers on my desk, wanting this discussion to be over.

"What about Ruben?"

I start to choke at her question, having just taken a sip of coffee.

"What about me?" Ruben asks, walking into the office. "Hey, Jacky. How's it going?" He sits in the spare visitor's chair across from my desk.

"I'm okay." She shrugs her shoulders. "I was just asking Sebastian if you wanted a woman," she blurts out to my stunned brother.

After a few moments, when Ruben still doesn't reply, I start to laugh. A woman has finally left my big, badass brother speechless. This is too good to be true.

Ruben turns his head and gives me a death glare, which used to work when we were kids, but not anymore. It just makes me laugh all the more. Seeing Jacky's face fall, I finally draw breath and compose myself, returning to the hotshot businessman I am.

"Jacky, why would you want to know if I wanted a woman? What makes you think I don't already have one? And what makes you think Sebastian here doesn't need one?" he smirks.

Hearing his last question, I hope Jacky doesn't pick up on it, because neither Ramon nor I have yet explained to our families that Carla is now with me.

"He has a woman." She stands up, straightens her clothes, and stomps out of the office, banging the door behind her.

Ruben frowns. "This woman. Is she real, or is she just to stop Jacky?"

I sigh, knowing I'm going to have to tell him something. "Yes, it's true."

He opens his mouth to say something, but nothing comes out, and he shuts his mouth again.

"It's been complicated. It's not so much now, but it's been hell because I thought she was with someone else. As it turns out, she wasn't really with him. The whole damn situation was driving me crazy." I drag a hand from the back of my neck over my head and down my face, exhausted. But my exhaustion now has more to do with the sexy-as-sin woman I can't do without.

"Carla," Ruben says with a wry grin. "I have eyes. As far as I know, you've been on your best behavior for months now. I've also seen you lusting after her when you thought no one was watching, and vice versa." He sits forward in his chair. "What I don't understand is her relationship with Ramon. If she wants you, why did they continue pretending?"

Itching to call Carla, I start fiddling with my phone while staring at my brother. "He told us about Gary the other day, didn't he? I think he'd had enough of Mom trying to marry us all off. I mean, it does get tiring." I shrug, leaning back in my chair. "I'm not really sure I understand Ramon's reasoning."

He nods and goes dark and thoughtful. There is something wrong at his club, and I wish he'd just tell me instead of prolonging the inevitable. I don't have all day, though. I have some paperwork for Jacky to handle over the next day or two while I'm with Carla, so I asked, "What are you doing here? I've been acting as CEO for about six months, and I can count on one hand the number of times you've been in here during that time."

He looked uneasy, looking anywhere but at me.

"Rosie was attacked in one of the restrooms at the club last night."

My eyes widen as I watch my brother stand and begin to pace back and forth in front of my desk. "She's all right. Keith got to her just in time to watch her knee him in the balls. Thank God. I tried to get her to move into my spare room, but she refused because I'm her boss. The pigheaded woman."

At this, I start to chuckle. "Are you sure your motive was purely honorable?" Unbeknownst to him, my brother has a thing for "Little Rosie," and watching them together is entertaining, to say the least.

He scowls, ignoring my comment. "She says she doesn't know the guy, but it's the same guy you saved her from on the dance floor the other night." Keith recognized him. I don't know what's going on at my own club, and it's pissing me off." He stops in front of my desk and looks at me. "I came here to see if you, Ramon, and Lucien could come to the club, act like you're drinking and catching up, and keep a lookout.

Something is going on, and I intend to find out what it is."

I nod. "That's fine, but I don't really want to get Carla into trouble. She's in enough as it is. I also don't want to leave her alone at night." I need to work something out to help him. "Leave it with me. I want to help you, so we'll see what can be worked out. Are you going to talk to the others?"

"Yeah, I'm heading over there now." Ruben started to leave, then looked back over his shoulder. "Thanks, Sebastian."

"Don't say anything to anyone about me and Carla just yet, okay?" I shout after him, and he acknowledges my request with a wave of his hand.

12

Carla

"OKAY, NOW IT'S JUST US FOR PROBABLY FIVE MINUTES. I want you to tell me about Sebastian," Lily insists, patting the cushion beside her. With a wicked gleam in her eye, she wants more than a few words. "Carla, I might be pregnant, but that doesn't mean I've lost my intuition or my eyesight." She grinned at me while smoothing her top over her huge stomach. "Besides, I'm not having sex right now, since Michael read online that a man's sperm can induce labor." She rolls her eyes. "I wouldn't mind labor starting. I look like an elephant, and it's damn uncomfortable."

I start laughing and collapse into the seat she pats.

"You're only a couple of weeks from your due date, right?" Seeing Lily nod, I continue, "Twins usually arrive early, so personally, I think you're doing really well holding on to them."

Lily rests her head back against the cushion before turning to look at me. "So, Sebastian."

I feel like squirming in my seat as she looks at me in that all-knowing way. "What do you want to know?"

She smirks. "Carla, I want to know everything. He's my brother-in-law, a fine specimen, and since I'm not letting Michael near me, I need secondhand information, and you're the only one here."

Thank God I'd already finished my coffee, or Lily's words probably would have choked me to death.

"I thought you said Michael wouldn't have sex with you." Are we really having this conversation? Unreal.

"He won't put his cock in me." I widen my eyes at her bluntness. Considering the topic of conversation, I should have been prepared for it. "But he keeps trying to put his mouth on me." She grins. "I told him that if he refused to use his cock, then my legs and mouth would stay closed."

I listen to her talk about her sex life, and then I start laughing. In fact, I'm laughing so hard that tears leak from the corners of my eyes.

There's no way she's going to let me off the hook, and since she knows there's something between us, I guess I won't give much away.

"Will you keep it to yourself for now, until we can tell Pippa?"

"I can do that. So spill."

She's infectious. "I've never been with Ramon the way everyone thinks. Something happened, and I agreed to pretend to be his girlfriend. I didn't expect to fall for his brother. I'm in love with Sebastian, and I think I have been since we first met at your wedding."

I turn my head to look at Lily. "We've been together these past three days. Today is the first day Sebastian has gone into the office since he showed up at my door." I offer a slight smile. "He didn't want to leave me, but he had a meeting he couldn't get out of."

After a few minutes, Lily breaks the silence. "I noticed his attraction to you at my wedding. He couldn't take his eyes off you. I've also noticed him watching you when he thinks no one is looking. In the time I've known him, he's never been like that before." Lily sighed. "To be honest, I was worried at first because I thought you were his brother's girl. But as I watched the two of you, I saw an electric attraction between you. With Ramon, you were always just friends. So, it's a relief to know there won't be any family conflict."

"There won't be any conflict, although it was difficult and upsetting to want to be with him but not want to break my promise to Ramon. It was more difficult for Sebastian because he thought I was sleeping with his brother. At least we're together now."

"Whose together now?" Lucien asked, striding into the room and going straight to Lily. He placed a kiss on her cheek. "You okay?"

"I'm fine, Lucien. I thought you were picking Sabrina up on your way here." Lily pushes him aside and spots her friend hovering in the doorway.

Something's going on here, and I think it's Sabrina and Lucien. She sure as hell doesn't look happy with Lucien fawning all over Lily, something the rest of the family is used to. Even Michael has accepted his brother's coddling of his wife. Lucien has spoken out on more than one occasion, calling her his sister. But

I guess Sabrina's absence hasn't helped her perception of their relationship.

Lucien sits opposite us and glares at Sabrina until she straightens up and joins us, sitting as far away from Lucien as possible without being rude. This gets a raised eyebrow from Lucien.

Sabrina completely ignores him, glancing between Lily and me but staying silent.

"How are you settling back into life in the States?" I ask, wanting to break the tension that arrived with them.

"Just fine. I love the cabin Michael found for me, and I love the peace and quiet of the area." She paused. "The weather here is a nice change because it rained for weeks before I left London. Anyway, enough about me. Lily, how are you feeling?"

I'm beginning to feel uncomfortable about the tension between Sabrina and Lucien. I wish I could be a fly on the wall when they're alone, but then again, maybe not, as it'd be an explosive encounter.

"I feel like an oversized elephant, and Michael refuses to do anything to induce labor."

Trying not to laugh at the freaked-out look on Lucien's face is easier said than done. It takes him a minute to compose himself before he asks, "How, dare I ask?"

I can't control the snicker that bursts from my lips. "You really shouldn't have asked that, Lucien."

He still looks clueless, but he won't be for long.

"A man's sperm can trigger labor when the due date is close, but Michael refuses to—well, you know —inside me." Lily grinned at Lucien, who looked damn uncomfortable now. "Lucien, are you feeling okay?"

Trust Lily to draw attention to his embarrassment.

"I'd rather not have that image in my head. Thanks for that," he says, standing up. "I think I'll leave you ladies to catch up." He bends down and kisses Lily again, then scowls in Sabrina's direction. Turning to me, he winks before walking out of the room.

Lily chuckles. "I think I went a bit too far with him, but it was fun. He doesn't normally blush," she says, looking at her friend, who ignores her.

"Lily, I need to head back to the city. I have some things to do," I say quietly, hoping to sneak off and avoid the tension in the room.

Lily takes my hand and pulls me in for an

awkward hug. "Seduce his socks off," she whispers in my ear.

I grin, say goodbye to a brooding Sabrina, and walk out of the living room. I bump into Lucien, Michael, and Elias and say goodbye to them before climbing into my car.

There's certainly a lot of family back and forth at Michael and Lily's house. As I pull away from the house and drive slowly down the lane toward the highway, I can't help but feel slightly envious of the McKenzie family's closeness. I love my own space, but it would be lovely to know I have family close by, something I hadn't missed until I started hanging out with them.

As I pull onto the highway, I start speeding up when I see a black SUV barreling toward me at high speed in my rearview mirror.

Trying to keep my nerves at bay, I continue driving at the legal speed, hoping the SUV will pass. But when I glance back, I see that it has slowed down and is now trailing behind me.

Could it be Gary? I can't make out the driver because of the tinted windows. How would he have gotten the money for such a fancy car? I'm stupid. I chide myself. Of course he stole it if it's him. Why isn't the driver passing me?

The car keeps weaving between lanes, but doesn't pass me. Then, I feel a jolt as the car pushes forward.

He bumped my car. My fingers clench the steering wheel as my stomach turns and panic sets in. As I watch the car pull back slightly, I reach for my cell phone, which I'd placed on the passenger seat, and hit speed dial two for Sebastian.

"Hey, babe," he answers immediately.

"Sebastian, I don't know what to do," I say, panicking. "There's an SUV following me, and they hit my bumper." I start to cry. "I'm frightened."

"Fuck, baby. Where are you?"

"I left Lily and Michael's about five minutes ago and am heading back to the city." I watch the SUV pull up to me again and clip my bumper, making me scream.

"Carla... Carla... Fuck, answer me, damn it," he shouts down the phone, sounding frantic. "I'm just calling Michael. Hang on."

"Okay, I'm here." I wipe the tears from my eyes. "There's no one around to help me."

I can hear Sebastian talking to someone in the background.

"Baby, I've called Michael. Dad and Lucien are on their way to you, and I'm leaving. I'm just getting into my car."

I heard his car door slam, followed by the screeching of tires. It will take him about twenty minutes to get here. I don't think I have time, as the SUV speeds up again.

"Sebastian," I cry. "I love you."

"Carla, don't you dare do this."

The SUV hits the back of my car at full speed, sending me spinning across the road toward the ditch.

"SEBASTIAN!"

Sebastian

As Carla screams, I feel like ten years have gone from my life. She means everything to me, and the thought of her being hurt and alone is killing me. I hit the gas and quickly leave the city behind. Once the traffic thins out, I speed-dial Dad and pray that he and Mom are with her.

"Dad—" I say, hearing my dad's voice.

"Carla's fine, son," he tells me before I can ask.

Everything becomes blurry, so I pull over and swipe at my eyes.

"Son, you there?"

"Yeah. What...what did you find?" I need to know what's going on. I put my head in my hands and listen to my dad describe the destruction of the car.

"It's completely destroyed," he says. "There's nothing but bent metal at the front of the car. She's damn lucky she can walk away from it. If you ask me, it was a combination of her seatbelt and airbag that saved her life. I've tried to call Ramon, but he isn't answering."

Ramon? Then I realize that my parents and my other brother have no idea what's been going on with Carla or that she's my sister.

"He's flying, Dad. I'm on my way and should be there soon. Can I talk to Carla?"

I sit in my car on the side of the road, letting the engine idle. I don't know how I'm going to react to hearing the voice of the woman I love.

"Lucien took her back to the house while I wait for the sheriff. She refused to let us call the EMTs and refused to go to the hospital, so we compromised. They're going to check her out at the house. Her shoulder hurts from the seatbelt, and she'll probably have bruises on one side of her face from smashing into the airbag. You'll see soon enough if you're on your way. I've got to go, son. The sheriff is just pulling up."

Fuck! He hung up on me.

Trying to calm down, I leaned back against the seat and closed my eyes, taking deep breaths. The last thing she needs today is for me to get involved in an accident. With that thought in mind, I pulled away and tried to keep my speed down, which was extremely difficult.

Gary needs to be taught a lesson. It's a lesson I wouldn't mind teaching the bastard. After today, Carla isn't going anywhere without someone with her, preferably me. Not even to the bathroom. My impatience to get to her starts eating at me, and I smack my fist against the steering column.

Before Carla, my life was one long party. Other than my family, I didn't take anything seriously, not even work. I'd blow it off time and time again for the chance to spend a few days with a new hot body.

Yeah, that was me—fast cars and faster women. Women who knew the score and wanted what my body could offer them.

But then I met Carla, and I realized that all I wanted was a woman to call my own. I wanted a woman to spend the rest of my life with, to bear my children, and most of all, I wanted a woman who would love me for myself and not because of the McKenzie name and money. Today, I nearly lost all that because of him.

He caused the accident that nearly killed her. He is going to pay for that when I get my hands on him.

I slow down, pull over to the side of the road, and roll the window down. I can't take my eyes off the wreck of Carla's car.

"Hey, Sebastian." I hear the sheriff, but I have trouble finding my voice. She could have been killed in that chunk of steel. "Sebastian? Are you all right?"

"No." I shake my head and finally drag my eyes away to locate the sheriff, Thomas Jefferson. Yeah, his parents loved history. "Did you catch the bastard?"

"Not yet," he says, leaning through the open window. "But I will."

Not if I find him first.

"Keep me in the loop, will you, Tom?"

"As best I can." He steps away from my car and stands back, watching me drive off.

As soon as I turn the corner, I floor it, praying that Carla is okay when I get there.

13

Carla

I'M SITTING ON THE SOFA IN THE LIVING ROOM OF LILY and Michael's home, and every bone in my body aches. Inside, though, I just feel numb. When my car started spinning out of control, Sebastian's face was all I could see, and my heart broke because I honestly believed I wouldn't survive.

Crashing the way I did was one of the most terrifying experiences of my life, right up there with being beaten within an inch of my life. Both events were caused by the same man. I wanted to see him dead and gone, which was unlike me, but he'd tried to take my life twice.

The thought of him trying again—which he will, after having failed twice—is causing my heart to race and a pain to lance my head. Fear courses through my body, more apparent than the pain of being thrown around in the car. What if Sebastian gets in the way? Knowing Sebastian, he will do anything to protect me —as will his brothers, by the sound of things.

I glance over at Lucien, his father, and Michael, who are arguing. I have no idea what they're arguing about, but Lucien looks pale.

In fact, when he pulled me out of the car, I wasn't sure who had been in the accident because he'd lost all color, and his hands were unsteady. I also noticed that his father was looking not just at me, but at Lucien as well. Once my befuddled brain started working again, I remembered that he'd been in a bad accident that left him scarred.

I wasn't the only one watching Lucien with concern, either. Five minutes ago, Sabrina had been standing in the doorway, Lucien the object of her gaze. She disappeared the minute he caught her watching him.

"Carla, can I get you anything else?" Pippa dragged my gaze away from the men and back to her as she passed me a mug of coffee.

I don't want anything other than Sebastian, but I can't tell her that because she has no idea that I've switched sons.

"No, not really. Thank you for your concern." I start sipping the coffee she handed me and notice the frown on her face.

"Honey, you don't need to thank me. I care about you. You're Ramon's girl. Why wouldn't I care about you? You're like family."

I feel bad watching her wipe a tear from her eye.

"I'm sorry, Pippa. I didn't mean to upset you. It's just that it's been me and my brother for a long time —well, when he's around—and sometimes it feels strange being part of a family again. Ramon keeps telling me that I'm part of his family." I smile, or at least I think I do. My whole body feels numb, and I'm not sure what I'm doing.

"Thank you for telling me. Please know you will always be welcome in my home, and I imagine in this one too, even if things don't work out with Ramon." Her face hardens now. "He should be here with you. If he knew you were in trouble like Lucien mentioned, then he shouldn't have left for business. He's going to have to answer to me when he gets home."

I snort. I know, very lady-like, but it makes Pippa

laugh, which sets me off, and I end up in tears. Pippa pulls me close and wraps her arms around me.

"Now, now, honey. You're safe now. My boys won't let anything happen to you." She strokes my hair down my back, which makes me cry harder. Being held tight in a mother's arms undoes me.

I cry for myself, for Noah, and for my parents. I cry for the heartache I know I've caused Sebastian, not just today when he heard the crash, but for all the time he spent being tormented by my relationship with his brother.

It feels like I've been crying for hours, but I've actually only been crying for about five minutes. My tears finally dry up, so I pull back, wipe my eyes, blow my nose, and offer Pippa an embarrassed smile.

"Why don't you go wash your face before the EMTs arrive? They should be here soon." Pippa pats my hand as I pull myself together and head to the guest bathroom, feeling my body ache even more.

After splashing cold water on my bruised face, I walk back to the living room, collect my coffee, and walk to the window to wait for Sebastian. I need his arms around me, holding me tight and telling me how much he loves me.

I know everyone in the room is watching me for

signs of a breakdown, but I've already had one and will probably have another one big time when Sebastian gets here. Hopefully, his family won't be too angry with us because, when he arrives, there won't be any doubt as to who I'm with.

"Are you feeling a bit better, Carla?" Pippa asks, coming to stand at the window with me.

Before I can answer, I hear a car screech to a halt outside. I flinch at the sound, fear lancing through me. But when I glance outside and see Sebastian jumping from the car, a small whimper of relief escapes my throat.

All I know is that the man I thought I'd never see again is here for me. I don't think. I slam my coffee mug down on the windowsill and walk as quickly as I can toward the front door, leaving Pippa stunned by my reaction.

I pull the door open just as Sebastian runs up the front steps. Seeing me standing there, his eyes fill with unshed tears. He walks toward me and takes my face in his hands, caressing me like a lover.

"Hold me," I whisper as his eyes run over me.

"I'm afraid I'll hurt you," he says, his voice hoarse with emotion.

I shake my head, reach up, break his hold on my

face, and wrap my arms around his neck. His arms go around my waist. He pulls me into his body and holds me tight as I start to cry into his neck.

"God, baby, I love you," he mumbles into my neck.

Sebastian

I finally have Carla in my arms, and I never want to let her go. My hands shake as I hold her tightly, tears flowing from my eyes onto her neck.

My family is probably witnessing our reunion and my breakdown, but I don't care. I almost lost the woman I love today. I pull her closer, stopping myself just in time from caressing her body to make sure it's all intact and perfect.

"Sebastian, I'm not sure what's going on, but you should come inside."

My mom. She'll want an explanation, and I don't blame her. I just wish we'd had the chance to tell her before she found out about us like this.

Unwilling to let go of Carla, I pick her up and carry her to an armchair. I sink down into it with her arms still wrapped around my neck, her face buried in my chest. I position her comfortably on my lap.

I take the handkerchief my father passes to me, wipe my face, and look around. Lucien smirks when I catch his eye. Dad looks just as stunned as Mom, and Michael looks delighted, probably because Mom has someone else to concentrate on for a while.

I clear my throat and sum up everything in a few short sentences, "I love Carla, and she loves me. She was only pretending to be Ramon's girlfriend, though I only found that out three days ago. Ramon can explain the reasoning behind it because I'm too tired to deal with all your questions right now. I just want and need to take care of my woman."

Mom takes a seat opposite and *really* looks at me. When she catches me watching her, she grins and asks, "So, another wedding?"

My eyes widen, and I feel Carla in my arms. What the hell. "Damn straight there will be, but not until I've spoken with Carla in private." I bend down and kiss the top of her head, holding her close.

Lucien comes over, squeezes my shoulder in support, and says, "At least your dry spell is over." He grinned as he started to saunter out of the room.

Mom gasps. "Lucien Elias McKenzie, come back

here right now! You're not too old to go over my knee."

Carla raises her head and starts to chuckle at Lucien, who is frozen in place, looking like a deer in headlights.

"Sorry," he mumbles. "I'm going to check on Lily. I promised to let her know how you are. She's going to love this revelation."

"You're an ass," Sabrina says, drawing all eyes to her. She blushes as red as a tomato, manages a gruff "I'm sorry," and turns to go in the opposite direction of Lucien.

Well, she rendered my brother speechless, which is a first.

Without another word, Lucien makes his way to the stairs and runs up them, sounding angry.

Carla sits up in my lap, uses the tissues Mom just gave her to wipe her tears, and meets my eyes. She smiles, then takes my face in her hands and seals our lips together. I'm hit by a bolt of electricity. Her wet, hot mouth against mine, her tongue seeking and finding mine, makes my pants go from comfortable to uncomfortable in five seconds flat.

She tastes divine—like my woman. I'm really struggling not to take over because I don't want to hurt her, but she's killing me. I'm seconds away from grabbing her hips and rearranging her so that I can rub against her. Unfortunately, the EMTs arrive and break us apart.

"Wow," I mutter, wondering how the hell I'm going to adjust my erection with everyone looking on. Before Carla can stand, we hear someone running down the stairs.

"Lily's in labor." Lucien's words cause utter chaos.

My mom screams, and Dad tries to hush her in annoyance. Lucien looks ready to pass out, and Sabrina rolls her eyes at his glazed look. The EMTs freeze, then start toward Carla again. She waves them away and points upstairs.

"Hey, babe. You need to have them check you out." The bruising on her face seems slight, only around her left eye and forehead. It isn't as bad as I thought. After watching her rub her temples, I'm also going to guess that she has a headache.

She climbs off me, holds out her hand, takes mine, and tries to get me to budge from the chair. When I don't move, she raises an eyebrow. "You staying here?" She grins and sticks out her tongue, slowly licking her red lips. I can't focus when she does that. This woman drives me to the brink of craziness. If my family weren't here, I'd already have her naked and buried between her legs.

Fuck. It's not good to have lustful thoughts while all hell is breaking loose.

"Don't worry. I'll get checked out at the hospital, since that's where we're heading anyway."

I'm not too keen on this idea. I'd prefer for her to be checked out as soon as possible. But, from what I can tell, the EMTs are going to take a stressed-out Michael and Lily to the hospital in the ambulance.

"Michael, please calm down. Women do this all the time," Lily chides. She comes down the stairs, supported by her husband and an EMT, who lead her to the ambulance. Mom and Lucien are fussing again.

Michael looks more in need of medical care than Lily does, with his hair sticking up all over the place and his complexion white as a sheet.

"I'll drive there. Mom, Dad, are you coming with me?" Lucien asks, running his hands through his already messy hair. Then, as an afterthought, he asks, "Sabrina, are you coming?"

"Of course."

God knows what my brother has done to piss her off. She's angry with him about something, and, if I'm honest, I can't wait to find out what kind of ass

Lucien's been. Coming back to my senses, though, I realize there is no way Lucien can drive. He's about as worked up as Michael.

I wrap an arm around Carla, whom I'm not prepared to let go of just yet, and lead her outside. I come to a stop beside my brother, snag the keys out of his floundering hand, and say,

"You can't drive. One crash today is one too many." I turn to my dad, who is always levelheaded. "Dad, you drive."

He catches the keys I throw to him. "Right. I think that's probably for the best." He turns to my mom, takes her by the hand, and drags her to Lucien's SUV. "Lucien, are you joining us?"

Carla pulls away from me, walks in front of my idiot brother, and, before I can say or do anything, lifts up and hugs him. He eventually returns the hug. "She'll be okay, Lucien. You know that, right?" she whispers to him. I just catch the last part.

He looks as though he's just come out of a trance. "Shit! Please tell me you're not going to have a baby anytime soon."

Carla chuckles. "Lucien, get with it. Go sit in your car and be nice to Sabrina."

He scowls at her, but walks over to his car and

opens the door for Sabrina. After a slight hesitation, she climbs in, followed by Lucien. I wish I were a fly on the wall during that car ride. I'm going to have to butter Mom up to find out what happened. She likes to gossip with the best of them, which I usually ignore. However, I might need to start paying more attention.

For now, though, I need to get my woman into my car and to the hospital, where she's going to get checked out.

14

Carla

I'M CURLED UP IN THE PASSENGER SEAT WHILE Sebastian drives us to the hospital. In all my years, I've never seen a man come apart the way Sebastian did back at the house, and I don't think I'll ever forget it. I now know what it feels like to be loved and cherished by a man. He wants to marry me. I thought I was hearing things when he told his mom and anyone else within earshot. My heart stuttered in my chest, filling with hope and longing. The man I was in love with wanted to make me a permanent part of his family.

Every now and then, he glances at me out of the

corner of his eye. I reach out and place my hand on his arm, slowly caressing down to his hand, which rests between us. After tracing each of his fingers with mine, I entwine our fingers together and stroke his thumb.

I just needed to touch him. I need to know this isn't a dream, that I'm really sitting beside him.

No words are exchanged, but none are needed as we're both comfortable with the silence. The silence also gives me time to watch him.

He has a strong jaw that already bears a hint of five-o'clock shadow. I slowly trail my eyes lower, taking in his broad shoulders encased in a white shirt. He always looks so professional in his business attire. I remember what he looks like underneath that shirt, and I feel an ache between my legs. I always ache when he's close, or even when I hear his voice. Sebastian has strong thighs with a light sprinkling of hair, and his manhood—oh boy! When he's aroused, he's thick and long. His hairless groin makes it so damn hot when I take his balls into my mouth and leave him shaking with pleasure.

As I watch him, I feel heat licking my body. He is divine, and I know he feels my gaze as the bulge in his pants grows before my eyes. Unable to help myself, I lick my lips, and then I look up at him when I hear him groan.

"If you keep looking at me like that, I won't be responsible for the consequences."

His hand tightens on the steering wheel, yet I can't seem to keep my eyes above his waist. What the hell is wrong with me?

I move into a more upright position and lean toward him, kissing his jaw before licking down his neck and leaving a trail of small bites.

"Carla," he groans in warning, which, of course, I take no notice of.

"Hmm, Sebastian. I've missed you."

My hand knows what it wants, and it wants to touch him. Stroke him. Give him pure bliss. I'm not sure about while he's driving, but I can tease him.

I slide my hand over his thigh and up. I reach the root of him and hear him inhale when I press lightly against his balls. Now that he's spread his legs slightly, I can reach them. I smile to myself. I watch my hand trace the length of his rigid erection, then back down. His legs quiver. I squeeze him, rubbing the tip through his pants, just as the car swerves, followed by a string of curses.

I remove my hand and sit back in my seat. "Sorry.

I got a bit carried away." I close my eyes so I won't be tempted to look at him.

"Carla, baby, it's okay. I got carried away too, and I love that you want me as much as I want you. I love having your hands on me."

I open my eyes to look at him.

He grins. "I love that you can't keep your hands off me. If we weren't driving, you'd be riding my dick while I had a mouthful of your breasts."

Groaning, I wiggle in my seat as Sebastian starts to laugh.

"The hospital is coming up. As soon as we get inside, you're going to get checked out, okay? Then, we'll go sit with our family."

Sebastian starts to turn into the hospital parking lot when I realize that he said "our family." He chuckles when he notices the look on my face.

"Carla, they are 'our' family. Even if nothing were happening between us, they would still be 'our' family. Don't you realize that Mom has fallen for you? On the days when you've gotten out of going to their place for dinner with Ramon, she always fusses about you not being there." He laughs. "Ramon has been nagged because of you."

"He never said anything. Why wouldn't he have

told me? I only avoided going because I was feeling down about my brother, and I didn't think I could handle seeing Sebastian."

"Don't worry. It was fun watching him squirm and try to explain without giving anything away." He jumped out of the SUV and ran around to my door. He opens the door, reaches in, and takes hold of my hand. "Ramon is brilliant at getting around Mom. When we were kids, he was always the one we nominated to ask permission for things. He always had an answer for everything." He chuckles. "Now, on that note, let's get you checked out before we go find out what's happening to Lily."

Sebastian

I can't take my eyes off Carla, who has been having a deep conversation with my mom ever since we arrived on the maternity floor.

I had to convince her to get the scan when she saw the doctor because she refused it. They wanted to check for internal bleeding. After pulling some strings, I managed to get the scan done within fifteen minutes of her finally agreeing to it. I've never used my wealth to get what I wanted before, but this time, for my woman, I pulled out all the stops and used all my connections to get things moving.

At least we know there is no internal damage from when she was restrained by the seatbelt and the airbag exploded in her face.

She has bruising under her clothes, as well as a black eye that has been forming since the accident. Seeing her all bruised up during the examination made me want to hunt the bastard down and show him what happens when he messes with my girl.

"What the hell are you thinking about, with that look on your face?" Ruben nudges me, standing beside me in the waiting room, having just arrived.

"The fucker who hurt Carla." I glance at him before looking back at her. "He's going to pay for what he's done to her, and he's not going to be able to harm her again."

"You love her."

It isn't a question, so I say nothing.

"Let me know if you need any help. Any help at all. You got me?" Serious Ruben doesn't appear all that often. "I know what it's like to want to protect someone from threats when you have no idea where the next one will come from."

I frown, listening to him, having no idea what he's talking about. When has he ever been in this kind of situation? I know he has trouble asking for help, but he wouldn't handle the issues at his club alone, would he?

Before I can ask him about it, Ramon comes running into the waiting area. He looks around, spots Carla getting to her feet, and walks over to pull her into his arms.

I hear her sniffling into Ramon's shoulder as he holds her tight. Standing against the wall near the window, I can't help but feel jealous. I try to fight it back and stay put, but my feet have a mind of their own, and I find myself standing next to them, rubbing Carla's back to calm her down. Ramon meets my eyes above Carla's head as she pulls away. Without wasting any time, I pull her into my side and kiss her on the head.

"Don't worry, brother. I know whose woman she is. But remember, she's like a sister to me, and I'll beat the crap out of anyone who hurts her. That includes you."

Carla gasps beside me, but I know where Ramon

is coming from. He knows about my history with women and my preference for one-night stands. Part of me wishes he could read my mind so he'd know just how much I'm in love with Carla. Another part of me is relieved he can't, considering the thoughts I've buried about what I want to do to her once she's recovered.

I also need to get the image of Carla's hands rubbing up and down my groin out of my head. If she hadn't been injured and it had been dark, I might have pulled over because I wanted her mouth on me badly.

"She's going to marry me. When I ask her," I say, stunning Ramon, who now looks like a fish out of water, opening and shutting his mouth without a sound.

Carla is looking up at me, beaming, and it takes everything I have not to throw her over my shoulder, carry her out of the hospital, and take her back to my place so I can have my wicked way with her.

Ugh! Now is not the time or place for arousing thoughts, but how can I not have them when she's here with me? Touching me. She tries to get her hand into the back of my pants, but I remove it when I hear Ruben snickering behind us. I ignore him and instead watch Michael walk toward us. He looks ready to pass out.

"Michael, is everything all right?" Mom asks, putting her arms around his waist. She's probably thinking she can keep him upright.

"Yeah," he whispers, settling his gaze on Lucien, who hasn't said anything since we arrived.

"Lily keeps asking for you," he tells Lucien. His voice gains strength from whatever emotion he's dealing with. "I could use you being in there as well. She's more concerned about me right now than she is about herself."

I have to turn away, seeing Michael close to tears.

As I watch Lucien stand and walk toward Michael, I notice Sabrina for the first time. She doesn't look too happy about Lucien's departure. Is she attracted to my brother? This isn't the first time I've noticed something going on between them.

"Hang on," Ruben interrupts. "If he's going in with you and Lily, then I am." He stands with his feet apart and his arms folded in front of him.

"Wait a sec," Ramon says as he moves to stand beside Ruben. "If these two are going in with you, then I am," he says, his lips twitching.

Carla starts to chuckle and moves away from me,

knowing what I'm about to do. I kiss her on the lips, wink, and walk to stand beside Ramon. "If these three idiots are going in with you, then I am."

I catch Carla rolling her eyes from the corner of my eye as I finish speaking. I keep my eyes focused on Michael, knowing that if I look at her, I won't be able to hold in my laughter anymore.

Yeah, we're acting like adolescents, but some light-heartedness is needed after the shit day we've had. We also need to loosen Michael up before he ends up in a hospital bed beside his wife.

"Follow me," Michael says, turning and starting to walk back the way he came. "But no one's looking at Lily's pus—" He pauses as we snicker. "—bits."

"So that's what it's called now," Ruben mumbles. Michael turns to look back at him over his shoulder and gives him a death glare. It shuts him up anyway.

I just pray that I won't regret trying to get to Michael by going into the delivery room.

15

Carla

I WATCH THE GUYS HEAD INTO THE DELIVERY ROOM, trying to outdo each other. I sit next to Pippa while Elias seems to be asleep beside her, his head leaning back on the sofa.

"Don't worry, Carla. They'll be back soon. There's no way they're going to stay in that room willingly with everything going on. They just wanted to distract Michael from worrying about Lily and his children."

Pippa now seems to be looking at me as though I'm an insect under a microscope. "So, you're in love with my son. A different one than I originally thought."

Not sure how to answer, I nod in agreement, unable to stop myself from chewing on my bottom lip. It's a nervous habit I've tried for years to kick but failed miserably.

Pippa takes my hand, drawing my attention back to her. "Carla, I've known from the start that you and Ramon weren't all that into each other." I frown. "A mother knows these things. You were both relaxed around each other, but you acted more like friends than anything else. I also noticed how Sebastian reacted to you."

She smiles. "It hurt me at first to know how tormented Sebastian was because he was falling for you, but he thought you belonged to his brother." She lets go of my hands, looks around the room, and then moves her eyes back to mine. "I think it did him good that you weren't available. He hasn't slept around since he met you."

"Pippa!" Elias growls beside her. Straightening up, he looks at her with wide eyes.

"Oh, hush up." She pats his arm before continuing. "Sebastian takes after his father, dipping it in lots of holes before finding a perfect fit."

Does she mean what I think she means? Can she? Elias flushes as red as a strawberry, confirming my suspicion that she is indeed talking about getting his cock wet.

I hear chuckling from behind, so I turn my head and meet Sabrina's watering eyes. She seems to be having trouble trying not to laugh, which causes my laughter to burst forth.

I'm not sure if I like thinking about Sebastian dipping his cock in plenty of holes, but hearing about it from his mother is hilarious. I guess she wanted to bring some much-needed laughter into the room.

"What I want to know is why everyone thinks that is so funny. How do you know you want to spend the rest of your life with someone unless it's a perfect fit?"

Of course, this comment has us all hooting with laughter.

I'm still wiping my eyes a few minutes later when Sebastian, Ruben, and Ramon walk out of the delivery suite, looking pale as ghosts. Ruben and Ramon plopped down into the room's armchairs, but Sebastian stopped and leaned against the wall, not taking his eyes off me.

I walk over to him, and as soon as I'm in arm's

reach, he grabs me and pulls me against his chest. He buries his face in my neck and just breathes.

I hold him as tightly as I can, giving him the comfort he obviously needs, and I caress his muscular back, feeling him quiver under my hands.

Finally, he lifts his head and looks at me. "The only kids we're having are those delivered by a stork!"

He's serious. This morning, I woke up having never discussed marriage or babies with anyone. Not only has he admitted wanting to marry me, but he's also talking about having children. If I weren't so in love with him, he'd scare the life out of me.

I lift up and kiss him slowly. It's a long, languid kiss that I don't want to break, but I know we have an audience.

"Hold that thought, baby," Sebastian whispers as he nuzzles my neck, drawing a groan from me. "God, you're driving me crazy." He presses discreetly against me, letting me know just how aroused he is. "This is what you do to me." He nibbles my ear. "Even before we were together, you had me hard as steel."

My hands fall to his hips, caressing his tight butt, while he holds my face in his hands and kisses me. My toes curl. The pulse between my legs throbs. I'm helpless the moment he touches me.

"You two have remembered where you are, right?" Ruben mumbles, clearly embarrassed to be standing next to us.

My first reaction is to pull back quickly, but Sebastian won't let me. He slowly pulls his lips away from mine, grins, takes a deep breath, and pulls me over to the sofa in the room.

Sebastian is like a drug. I crave my next fix of him. As he settles me on the sofa, I lie down with my head in his lap, facing inward toward his stomach. He cups my head, holding me against his aroused body. I can feel him against my cheek. Hard and solid.

As I start to drift off to sleep, I hear Pippa ask why Lucien hasn't come out of the room yet.

Sebastian

With Carla asleep in my lap, I'm having a hard time getting my erection to subside. It wouldn't be such a problem if she were facing outwards, but with her face resting against it, I can't stop thinking about her mouth wrapped around me.

I stop stroking her hair and tangle my fingers in her flowing locks. She's beautiful. I was serious when I said she was going to become my wife. It was a bit presumptuous of me, but I figured that if she heard it out loud, she'd have fair warning of my intentions.

The fact that someone was trying to harm her because of her brother tears me in two. She doesn't deserve this. But then again, does anyone deserve to have a madman after them?

I drag my hand through my hair and look around the waiting room, which is full of my family and Lily's friend Sabrina. Sabrina hadn't looked happy when Ramon told Mom that Lily refused to let Lucien out of the room.

Their relationship will seem strange to anyone looking in, but we've just gotten used to seeing them interact. Thankfully, Michael has finally gotten over his jealousy.

Ramon walks over from where he was sitting with Sabrina and sits down across from us without taking his eyes off the woman in my lap.

"I've received a text from security at my building." He pauses. "Someone's been hanging around. It's Gary. They managed to pull a picture from the surveillance cameras, and it's him." Ramon leans back in his chair and crosses his ankle over his knee.

"I don't know why he's so obsessed with harming Carla. I know he's angry with Noah, but there's no reason to go after Carla like this."

I check to make sure Carla is still asleep before asking, "What did Noah do to make him this way?"

"He found out that Gary was selling drugs, so he told a friend of his who works in the drug squad." He shrugs. "They arrested him, but because of a technicality in the case, he was granted bail. He obviously fled after attacking Carla in Canada and showed up here."

Carla moves slightly in her sleep, pressing against my groin. She's driving me crazy without even realizing it.

"I'm not leaving her side, Ramon. I had a meeting today that I couldn't get out of, but from now on, she's staying with me."

Ramon starts to shake his head. "Sebastian, your apartment isn't as secure as mine. We've already discussed this," he says, holding his hand up before I can object. "But you can stay with her in my apartment for as long as you need to. I'm planning on sleeping at your place," he says, grinning. His grin turns into a frown as he looks behind me.

I turn my head and see Lucien standing just outside the delivery suite, looking sick.

"Lucien? Please say something."

He shakes his head as though to blow cobwebs away, then wipes his hand down his face in exhaustion.

Then he grinned. "Michael Elias McKenzie arrived eleven minutes before his sister, Charlotte Lily McKenzie, followed. Lily is doing great, as are the babies. But I'm not too sure about Michael," he chuckles.

Amidst all the cheers and questions flying out of Mom's mouth, Carla stirs. She moves her head to see what the fuss is about, then looks back at me with questions in her eyes. "Lily's had the babies, and everyone is doing well." I caress her face as she lies in my lap.

"I dreamt about you. About what I want to do to you," she says in a sleepy voice, then quickly bites down on my straining erection.

She sits up, keeping one hand on either side of me on the sofa, and leans in to nibble along my lips. She seals our mouths together and wraps her tongue around mine. I groan, trying to stop my hips from arching up into her. She's so fucking delicious. I need her naked and riding me.

Gripping her hips, I pull her onto me and push her material-covered pussy against my throbbing dick. I hold her still while we attack each other's mouths.

"Will you two go get a room already? Geez, bro. After that display, I'm going to have to go get laid," Ruben grumbles, making Carla laugh into my neck. I frown, refusing to show how funny I find his declaration.

Finally, Carla climbs off me, leaving the bulge in my pants on display. Ruben glances down, meets my eyes, and smirks.

"I'd pull the shirt out." With that comment, he starts walking toward the doors that everyone seems to have disappeared through. "We're going to take a quick look at our niece and nephew before leaving to let Lily get some rest." As he's about to push through the doors, he pauses and says, "Personally, I want to see how Michael is faring." He chuckles.

Carla holds her hand out to me. I take it, allowing her to pull me up so that I'm standing in front of her. She then reaches out and smooths her hand down the front of my shirt. "I love you," she says softly.

16

Carla

AFTER THE DAY WE'VE HAD, LYING ON THE SOFA IN Ramon's apartment with Sebastian feels like the most natural thing in the world. Unbeknownst to anyone, Lily had been in labor for some time before letting Michael and, consequently, everyone else know. This soon got her on her way to the hospital when her water broke.

I smile, remembering the look on Sebastian and his brother's faces when they first saw the newest additions to the McKenzie family. They were in awe of the two little bundles of joy.

Lily looked exhausted yet elated, and Michael

looked ready to fall over. I certainly didn't know what to make of Sabrina and Lucien. I wasn't the only one to notice, either.

Sabrina was sitting in one of the chairs cuddling Charlotte while Lucien practically hung over her, stroking Charlotte's head. Neither of them noticed Ruben taking their photograph. They stayed like that for about five minutes until Lucien broke the spell. He went to hug his brother, then kissed Lily, and left the room.

I've waited all day to be alone with my guy, and I can't wait any longer, whether he's asleep or not.

I slip the buttons on his shirt open and slide my hands inside, caressing his smooth abs and ribs. I shift slightly and glance up. Sebastian is watching me through heavily lidded eyes. "You enjoying yourself?"

"Hmm." Sitting between his thighs, I take in the sight of him lying sprawled out on the sofa at my mercy. His chest and groin are deliciously hairless, with just a sprinkling on his thighs. I love touching him and want to touch more of him.

I reach for his belt and zipper, but he stops my hands. "Baby, let's go to bed." He hisses when I grab his cock through his pants. "Fuck. Stop. Ahhh," he pants.

I bite him up and down through his pants, and he reacts. He tosses his head back and clenches his jaw as I stroke him with one hand. He unbuckles his belt while I pull down his zipper, freeing his dick. He lets out a low groan as I begin stroking him more firmly. I feel him grow harder in my hand. With a mischievous smile, I lean in and whisper, "You like that, don't you?" Then, I blow on the tip of his penis.

"God, yes!" he hisses, shuddering.

Maintaining his gaze, I lean forward and lick his penis from base to tip. His eyes darken as he watches me run my tongue around the head and taste him. It's sexy, and I groan with him, needing him between my legs.

"Naked. Now," Sebastian jumps up from the sofa, and lets his pants fall around his ankles before kicking them off. His shirt flies through the air, and he's naked while I'm still standing in front of him, fully clothed.

One lift of his eyebrow is all it takes to get me moving, and my clothes fly in the same direction as his.

I stand naked in front of Sebastian as he takes in the view and his cock starts to twitch. I'm so aroused that I'm wet between my thighs and my breasts ache for his touch. As if reading my mind, Sebastian takes two steps forward, reaching out to caress my collarbone and breasts. He cups them in his hands and rubs my nipples with his thumbs. I fall back on my heels, shut my eyes, and enjoy the sensation of his hands on me. He brings my arousal to fever pitch.

One hand slowly moves down over my ribs and belly, slipping between my legs and opening my folds. His finger slides deeper. "Baby, you're wet for me." He moves even closer, wrapping his arm around my back and pulling my chest flush against him while slipping his finger inside my soaking pussy.

He kisses my nose, then lowers his head to take one of my nipples into his mouth and suck it while his finger slides deeper. I shiver with need. If he weren't holding me up, I'd be on the floor. He sucks my nipples, switching between the two. His eyes meet mine, burning brightly as our breathing deepens.

Realizing that I'm being taken, I reach between our bodies and stroke the crown of his penis. He growls and starts pushing his fingers inside me faster and faster until I feel like I'm about to explode.

I wrap my hand around him and start moving it back and forth. Back and forth, caressing the head on the upward motion. His movements become more urgent, matching the rhythm of my hand--the intensity between us builds.

Sebastian releases my breast and pushes my hands away from his cock. "Come to me," he says, pressing his lips to mine and swallowing my tongue. His words are all it takes for me to erupt, the tension in the air exploding. I moan long and deep into his mouth, grasping his shoulders. He pushes me onto the sofa and kneels behind me. He presses my hands against the top of the sofa. "Hold tight," he whispers in my ear.

In one swift motion, he impales me on his cock, driving me into orgasmic pleasure. I rub my ass against his groin, feeling him swell and move frantically. *"Fuck, Carla! Fuck!"*

Another orgasm rushes toward me like a freight train. Sebastian thickens and lengthens as he slams into me one last time. He stays still as his cock twitches and ejaculates inside me, coating my walls. I come undone again and begin squeezing him. I squeeze every drop out of him as our orgasms erupt. I feel him shiver and collapse on top of me, exhausted and satisfied. He turns and falls back onto the sofa, leaving me impaled on his semi-erect penis, which then slips out.

"You're not going anywhere," Sebastian tells me as I try to move away.

"I'm uncomfortable like this."

"Then turn around." He helps me turn around and straddle him, pulling me in against his chest.

I snuggle down against him when we hear his phone buzz with a text message. I watch him reach behind him to the table to retrieve it.

He pauses slightly in his caresses of my back, so I ask, "Who is it? Is everything okay?"

After a minute, he replies, "Just business."

Why do I get the feeling that he isn't being totally honest with me? He can't be lying to me, especially after what we just shared.

"Carla, I promise it's nothing to worry about. Stop overthinking." Then his stomach growls. "Okay, I think I need a different kind of food to sustain me through tonight's carnal pleasures."

Carnal pleasures? What guy says that? Well, apparently mine does!

Sebastian

As I toss the salad to accompany the burgers cooking on the grill, I watch Carla out of the corner of my eye. She's damn sexy, walking around the kitchen in my shirt and showing off her legs. Depending on where she stands, I can see her silhouette through the shirt. It's no wonder my erection is trying to burst from my partially fastened pants.

"Are the burgers ready yet?" she asks, rubbing her hand up and down my back, causing my arousal to intensify.

I drop the salad tongs, turn around, and kiss her. Not just a normal kiss, but a kiss that speaks of possession. Gripping her hips, I lift her up and sit her on the countertop, stepping between her spread thighs. I smooth back the hair covering part of her face and tell her, "You are the most beautiful woman I've ever met." I kiss her eyelids. "You're mine." I grin and kiss her on the nose. "But most of all, you have my heart, and I'm yours. Always, babe. Always." Then, I seal our mouths together in the sweetest kiss I've ever given anyone.

Carla breaks the kiss first, tears in her eyes. She tells me, "That's the sweetest thing anyone has ever said to me. I love you, Sebastian, but I think the burgers are burning." She chuckles.

I quickly dash to the grill, remove the burgers, and toss them onto the plate Carla hands me. Not before she gives my ass a grope.

"You like?" I smirk.

"Oh yeah." She touches me again. "It's so firm and round. It makes me want to bite it."

"You need to stop unless you want me to take you on the kitchen floor."

I move away from her, trying to regain control, which I seem to lose whenever she's close. I take the burgers and salad to the dining table.

Carla sits in the chair I pull out for her, but not before I see her smirk at the bulge in my pants.

"Behave. Food first...then *cream*."

Her eyes widen when she figures out what I'm referring to, and I roar with laughter. She's so easy to tease, and she's so damn adorable when she is.

Another thing I love about this woman is her appetite. She's no lettuce leaf girl. Her burger is loaded with more stuff than mine, and that's saying something. I'm not even sure she's going to be able to fit it in her mouth. Then again, I could be wrong. My mouth hangs open as I watch her stretch her jaw and bite through the burger. She seems to struggle to chew with her mouth closed, so she puts the burger back on her plate, covers her mouth, and chews behind her hand. When she meets my eyes, her laughter is evident.

"You enjoying that?" I laugh before taking a bite of my own.

"Damn straight. I didn't realize how hungry I was until I had this in front of me." She takes another big bite while I try to keep my mind off body parts. Body parts that want to be in that sexy-as-sin mouth.

Deciding to follow suit and refuel, I start shoveling my burger into my mouth, but I don't taste anything. I wait impatiently for Carla to finish eating.

"Hmmm, this is so good. I can't remember the last time I had a burger. Ramon prefers pizza and Italian food, whether we eat out or in," she mumbles around a mouthful of food.

She groans in pleasure at the food, and my senses go into overdrive. It would be great to have her moaning under me.

After taking a drink of water, I watch her for a few minutes before tactlessly telling her, "I've never met a woman who enjoys food as much as you do."

She freezes and raises an eyebrow. "Are you trying to tell me something?"

Oh, fuck!

"I didn't mean—I wasn't getting at—oh, hell!" I stand up, walk around to her chair, and crouch down. "Baby, I love every inch of you, and I love that you eat instead of starving yourself. If you starve yourself, then the curves that I love to touch would disappear."

"Nice save," she says, wiping her mouth with the napkin before placing it back on the table. "But I think you need to make it up to me."

I grin and pull her up with me. I toss her over my shoulder and run to the bedroom, where I drop her onto the bed.

"Christ, I'm going to be sick if you keep tossing me around when I've just eaten." She puts her hand to her stomach. I have a great view of her naked pussy, barely covered by my shirt.

Licking my lips, I drop to my knees, grab her thighs, and bring her to the edge of the bed. As I place her legs over my shoulders, I gently caress her from knee to hip. Each time I move closer to her hips, she arches into me, craving my touch elsewhere.

Within minutes, she's wriggling out of the shirt,

throwing it to the side of the bed, and offering me a huge grin. "You have access to all of me now."

"Oh, babe, I had access to all of you anyway." Without giving her time to think, I kiss her right on her pussy lips, setting her off wiggling around. Sliding my tongue through her folds, I taste her. Hearing her moan makes my dick hard as steel, and I'm not sure I'm going to last. She's a feast for the eyes, lying on the bed while I eat her pussy. Looking up slightly, she's watching me, and...and...fuck. She's tugging at her hard nipples.

My hips arch involuntarily against the side of the bed, causing an intense pleasure to start at the tips of my toes and move up my legs as my balls draw tight into my body.

Carla continues to play with her breasts and nipples. She arches up from the bed when I shove two fingers inside her to check her readiness. Boy, is she ready!

I quickly rise from the floor, practically ripping my zipper to free my cock, and thrust inside her, my balls slapping against her ass. I'm inside her that quickly.

"Oh God, baby. I can't go slow. I need to move." Before I can finish speaking, I start sliding in and out of her. Her walls grip my dick tightly. She's so warm, so tight, and so fucking wet.

"Ahhh." I start ejaculating, feeling her walls clamp down on me as she grinds against my groin during her climax. She's still squeezing me. She's milking every last drop of cum from my cock.

I drop down, resting my head in the crook of her neck as I try to catch my breath. Carla tightens her arms and legs around me, holding me close.

"I love you, Sebastian."

My whole body quivers at her words. I slide out of her, pulling her closer before rolling onto my back and pulling her on top of me.

"I love you too, babe. You make me feel and act like a teenager. I'm just so glad you came with me. It would have destroyed me to climax without you."

"Hmm, oh, I came. The minute you start releasing inside me, I always come. It's hot." Carla snuggles more into my arms, and I hear my cell buzz with two text messages, one after the other.

"Do you need to answer them?" she asks, half asleep.

She starts moving to the side to let me up. I quickly kiss her before climbing out of bed and padding across the floor to retrieve my phone. The whole time, I'm praying it isn't more texts from Jacky.

I have no idea what she's doing, but I'm definitely going to talk to her when I'm back in the office.

When I pick up my phone, I see that both texts are from Jacky. One is a picture message titled "What you're missing." Before I can delete it, the picture opens to reveal a naked Jacky standing in front of a mirror.

I quickly press delete and add her to the top of my mental calendar under "different department" or "different company." I'd prefer the latter, but I blame myself for leading her on in the first place.

Walking back into the bedroom, I see that Carla is curled up on her side, fast asleep.

17

***

Carla

I'M DREAMING. THERE'S A GOD ON TOP OF ME, MAKING sweet love to my body. He slides in and out of me, causing delicious friction.

Then the God says, "Wake up, Carla. I want you to be awake when I come inside you." I open my eyes and am met by a grinning Sebastian.

I start to giggle but end up groaning when he sucks a nipple into his mouth and massages it against the roof of his mouth with his tongue.

He lets it plop out of his mouth. "You were so sexy lying there uncovered. Your legs were spread, showing me your glistening pussy. I couldn't resist you."

"Hmm, I was dreaming that a god was making sweet love to me. I guess I was right."

I start to wrap my legs around his hips, but he stops me. Keeping his cock inside, he straddles my legs, making my channel tight.

He continues to move, more like a rocking motion. I stretch my arms out behind me, arch my back, and start coming apart in a slow burst of delicious tingles. My channel clenches and releases Sebastian's gliding cock, setting his release off.

"Carla," Sebastian groans, holding still.

When I feel him start to calm down, he drops his forehead against mine. "It's never been like that before. Never."

He slides out of me, then pulls me into his arms as our legs tangle.

"That was amazing. I could get used to waking up like that."

He chuckles. "Oh, you could. Could you?"

I kiss his chest. "Most definitely."

Lying in his arms makes all my worries disappear and replaces them with happiness. It gives me a future to hold on to, even though the crap of my past keeps interfering.

I fear the worst with Gary. He won't stop unless he's stopped, and I'm terrified that someone else will get caught in the crossfire.

I hold on to Sebastian even tighter and try to shut my mind down so I can relax and fall asleep. But I don't think that's in the cards for this morning.

"You're thinking too hard," Sebastian mumbles with his eyes closed.

I rise up and rest my chin on his chest. "I'm scared, Seb. I think Gary is going to come after me again, and I'm afraid you or someone else will get hurt trying to protect me." I try to blink away the tears, but Sebastian catches them with his thumbs.

"I'm not going to let anything else happen to you." He pulls me back down onto his chest. "He's not going to get the chance to hurt you because from now on, you won't go anywhere without me or one of my brothers."

"But—" I try to interrupt.

"My brothers and I grew up fighting," he chuckles. "And I don't just mean with each other. Dad had a couple of bags that we helped him string up in the barn, and we used them a lot. The McKenzie men have a temper. So don't worry that pretty little head of yours over us. We can take care of you and ourselves just fine, babe."

Although listening to Sebastian does reassure me somewhat, there's still the worry at the back of my mind that Gary will get to me or them.

"Tell me about him." He asks, stroking my back, then lingering on my butt.

"You really want to hear about him?" I lift my head to look at him.

"Not really," he says, his hand tightening on me. "But it might help to know what he's like."

I'm not too sure about that, but I decide to start with my brother.

"All my life, I've been good. First, I did what my parents wanted. Then, after they died from smoke inhalation in a fire at our house, I did what Noah wanted. Anything to keep the peace."

"I had no idea your parents died in a fire."

"They weren't supposed to be there. When the fire started, Noah got me out of the house, wrapped us in a blanket, and we watched the house burn. An hour later, we found out that our parents had been in the house. I catch a tear on its way down my cheek.

"Noah has always lived with the guilt that he didn't save them. That he left them to burn. It wasn't his fault. They told us they were staying in the hotel overnight where the reunion was being held. I guess something changed, but we never found out what. They'd left their car at the hotel, so we figured a taxi had brought them back to the house."

I kiss Sebastian's chest, trying to get closer to him. He makes me feel so secure when I'm wrapped tight in his arms.

"Noah had just finished college and used the insurance money to take care of us. He put me through school. He gave up a lot for me, and now he's out there, and I don't know if he's safe."

Sebastian puts his hand under my chin, lifts my face to his, and gives me a sweet kiss. "I'm sorry you both had it rough, but please tell me how Gary fits into all this."

I nod and rest against his chest again. "I met Gary in college, and we had an on-again, off-again relationship. Noah never liked him and kept telling me to steer clear. We kind of fizzled out, and then a few years went by. One night, I bumped into him at a club with friends, and I guess one thing led to another, and we started seeing each other again."

It's clear that Sebastian doesn't like this story, as he's started to tighten up.

"He was more possessive than he had been in the past, but I didn't think much of it at first, until he started threatening me. That's when I broke up with him and told him to stay away. He would have attacked me then and there if Noah hadn't walked in when he did. Not long after, Noah discovered that Gary was heavily involved in drugs, not just as a user but also as a distributor. He informed a friend in the drug squad about Gary, and they set up a sting operation. Gary got out on bail and came looking for Noah but found me instead. He used me as his punching bag."

I close my eyes, trying to block out the memories of his fists raining down on me. I shudder and continue, "That's how I ended up here. Noah had been working with Ramon, so I came down here, but Noah was gone. Ramon took me in. I found out that he'd already hired a private investigator to find Noah. It made sense for me to live with him, so we told everyone we were involved to keep people off Ramon's back. Plus, he didn't want people to get the wrong idea about me if he wasn't seemingly committed to me. Here we are. I'm lying in bed with the man I love, and I really don't want to get up. But we promised to visit Lily today, so we need to shower and get breakfast."

"You've left me speechless, baby." He kisses my nose. "I need to think about what you've said, and I'll talk to Ramon about increasing the search for Noah."

Sebastian slowly kisses my cheeks and each of my eyes, and I melt into him with a sigh. Suddenly, Sebastian flips me onto my back, looms over me, and offers me a wicked grin before sealing our lips together.

Sebastian

Lily has a private hospital room, not because of Michael's wealth, but because she had twins. My brother sounded worn out when I spoke to him this morning, which doesn't surprise me given that he hasn't slept the past few nights due to worry about his wife and the arrival of the twins, who need to be fed.

Going into the delivery room yesterday to see Lily was a huge mistake. Seeing her in so much pain almost made me throw up, and it made me realize it must be ten times worse for Michael and almost as bad for Lucien.

Not wanting to appear weak, I waited patiently for the nurse to kick us out, which she did after looking at Ruben, who looked green. At least he looked worse than I did, which made me smile.

"Hey, what are you grinning at?" Carla asked, squeezing my hand.

"I was thinking about how green Ruben turned when he saw Lily in the delivery room yesterday. My tough-as-nails brother nearly keeled over. It was funny as hell, and it's something I'm going to enjoy teasing him about." I laugh.

Carla rolls her eyes. "Boys will be boys."

I quickly pick her up and kiss her passionately before setting her back down. She's so cute with the blush I put on her face.

I chuckle as I open the door to Lily's room and drag Carla inside with me. We find Lily sitting up in bed, cradling both babies in her arms, supported by pillows. There's no sign of Michael, though.

"I made him go home to shower and change. He'll be back soon. I'm sure of it," Lily tells us, smiling and practically glowing with happiness.

Carla releases my hand and walks to one side of the bed. "How are you feeling?"

Reaching out, she strokes Charlotte's cheek, unable to reach Michael Jr.

"I'm fine." A bit sore, but what did I expect after pushing these two out? I guess I should be thankful that I had twins, because Michael said that we aren't having any more children after the experience he had yesterday." She snickers. "I mean, it wasn't as though he had to carry them for nearly nine months or go through all that pain. It was all worth it, though. In case you're wondering, Sebastian."

I wince. "Can we not talk about the delivery? I just ate."

"Ignore him, Lily, and please tell me I can cuddle one of your babies."

"You sure can. Would you like to take Charlotte, as she's the closest?"

Carla moves in and gently takes Charlotte into her arms before sitting back in the armchair next to the bed.

I watch as Carla snuggles Charlotte closer and gets lost in the baby. Suddenly, I realize that I want what Michael has. I've already told everyone that I intend to marry Carla, and then we can talk about having babies. I'm not sure how I'll get through her labor, but I won't let Michael outdo me. At least the twin gene is from Lily's side of the family, not the McKenzies'.

Looking back toward Lily, I see "that look" in her eyes. The same one Mom always wears when she's scheming.

I laugh. "Lily, you can get that look off your face. You missed it yesterday, but I've already announced to the family that I plan on marrying Carla." I meet Carla's eyes. "But I'll be asking in a setting she won't ever forget."

I hear sniffling and turn back to see Lily crying. "That was so gorgeous. I knew you just needed the right woman to get you on the straight and narrow."

Carla starts laughing. "Oh, he's on the straight and narrow now."

"Lily, what's wrong?" Michael asks as he comes into the room and dashes to his wife.

"Your brother."

Michael straightens up and looks at me as though he wants to put me in a headlock.

"Fuck! Um, Lily. You might want to rephrase that."

"Sorry," she chuckles. "Michael, your brother has

finally found 'the' woman for him." Michael still looks clueless.

"What Lily is trying to tell you is that I'm planning on marrying Carla once I've proposed."

"You're serious," he says, taking his son from Lily before sitting beside her on the bed. "Wow, I bet Mom's already planned your wedding," he laughs, turning to Carla. "You have to be firm with her, Carla. Tell her she can help, but it's your wedding. Otherwise, she'll completely take over. She won't mean to. She'll just get carried away."

"I'll remember that." Pause. "Sebastian, come say hello to your niece."

Okay. Why does that thought make me want to run out of the room?

Michael roars with laughter. "Brother, you're not afraid of a little baby, are you?"

"Of course not!" I scoffed, scared shitless.

Ignoring Michael, I walk over, perch on the arm of Carla's chair, and take my first proper look at Charlotte. She looks like her mom with dark hair and freckles on her nose. I wrap my arm around Carla and caress Charlotte's head. She's beautiful, and I'm not biased just because I'm her uncle. Well, maybe a little bit.

"I never thought I'd see the day when you went gaga over a baby." Michael cuddles his son between himself and Lily while watching Carla and me.

"I've never been an uncle before, so there's no need for it. Besides, I kind of like the idea of a baby girl. Perhaps we could keep Charlotte. That way, I won't have to go through what Michael did," I tease—he's my brother so what does he expect?

"You can have your own, because I want you to know what it's like to watch your babies come into the world. Although, I had to try to forget that they come out of the same place where we shove our... well, you know," he finishes lamely after receiving a glare from Lily, just as Mom pushes her way through the door.

"Michael, I hope you weren't about to say what I think you were."

"No ma'am," he groans, then bends and kisses Lily.

Unable to resist, I kiss Carla's neck and feel a shiver run through her. After Michael went on about women's parts, I couldn't get Carla's out of my head, nor could I forget what it felt like to be sheathed to the hilt inside her.

"Carla, let's go for a walk and get coffee, and let Granny have some time with the babies."

"Okay," she says as she passes Charlotte to my mom, who is hovering nearby. She then stands and lets my mom sit in her seat.

"We'll be back soon."

I practically drag Carla out of the room, followed by Michael's laughter.

18

Carla

WHAT HAS GOTTEN INTO SEBASTIAN? HE PRACTICALLY dragged me out of Lily's room, and now he's pulling me down the hallway as if there were a fire. He looks through a window at a room. "In here," he says, pushing the door open and pulling me inside before I can see what's going on.

"Sebastian—"

He slams his mouth to mine, pushing me up against the wall. Grabbing my thighs, he hoists me up, causing my legs to wrap around him. I come into contact with his huge, swollen cock, which makes my eyes widen. I had no idea he was so aroused.

I shove my fingers into his hair and hold his mouth to mine. The things he does with his tongue have me wet and aching.

"I need you, babe."

He lets my feet hit the floor, unzipping me and shoving my jeans and thong down my legs. He releases his cock, which is already wet at the tip. I can't take my eyes off him as he jerks with arousal, taking hold of himself and pulling back to the root.

"Carla," he says between gritted teeth. "I'm going to come the minute I get inside you."

That's the only warning I get. He spins me around. I place my hands on the wall as he pulls my hips toward him and thrusts inside me. He feels real good filling me up, setting off little electric shocks along my channel.

He lets go of my hips, wraps me up in his arms, slides his hands up inside my top, and shoves my bra above my breasts. He starts massaging and pinching my nipples.

"Hmm," I moan, resting my head on his shoulder.

My breath catches when he pulls almost all the way out, leaving just the tip inside.

"I'm going to fuck your cunt now."

Oh God!

He starts pumping his hips in and out of me. One hand stays on my nipple while the other moves to my clit. The minute he touches me between my legs, he pinches my nipple, and I explode. I see stars and can't stop climaxing. My channel grips Sebastian's cock. My muscles ripple up and down the length of him.

He pulls out, cursing, and shoves his fingers inside me so I can ride out my orgasm. I feel his other hand take hold of his cock, which is pressed against my ass. I turn my head and watch him ejaculate on the floor.

Unable to catch my breath, I rest against the wall while he removes his fingers from inside me. I hear Sebastian put himself back together, then bend and pull my thong and jeans back up. He turns me around to fasten them.

He kisses my lips and pulls me back into his arms. "God, I needed you, but it would have been too messy if I came inside you here."

"I know."

He quickly cleans up with some tissue before tossing it into the trash.

I love it when he comes inside me. It makes me feel more connected to him than just having his penis inside me.

He wraps his arms around me. "You like my

words, baby?" he whispers into my ear, rubbing my ass and pushing me against him.

"You can't be ready to go again?"

"I'm always ready with you. Answer the question," he chuckles.

I don't know why I blush when he uses those naughty words, but I do, and now I probably look like a tomato.

"You're not saying anything, but I'll let you off the hook for now because I know you find them as hot as I do when I use them. I bet if I touch your pussy, it'll be wet—and not just from the orgasm you just had."

Breaking away from him, I smack his arm. "Stop embarrassing me." I try to leave the room, but he catches me around the waist.

"I'll use those words again the next time I'm buried deep inside you," he whispers in my ear. "Your little cunt will tell me how much dirty talk turns you on."

My body feels alive again. He just brought me to orgasm, and I already need him again. His words turn me on, although I'm not used to hearing them in reference to my body parts. I've seen them in enough books. Hearing those words turns me on like crazy.

He stands in front of me and smirks when he sees

the lust I'm struggling to hide. If we weren't in an unlocked hospital room, I'd be all over him again.

"Come on, before Mom comes looking for us. I promise to behave in public from now on," he says, smirking.

He opens the door for me, and we walk straight into Michael and Lucien.

"Where have you two been?" Lucien pauses, looks between the two of us, and then continues, "Never mind. Carla, go back into Lily's room while we interrogate Sebastian. Don't worry, we're going to sit right over there by the door." Lucien points.

I offer an embarrassed smile, having been caught with my hand in the cookie jar, so to speak. "Um, okay. You'll save some for me, right?" I ask his two grinning brothers.

"Maybe," Lucien laughs. "Get in there and save Lily from Mom."

"Okay, I'm going." I walk into Lily's room to the sound of male laughter and find Pippa cooing over her grandchildren and telling Lily how to feed her babies.

I smirk when Lily rolls her eyes over Pippa's head. Pippa is a wonderful mom, and she's going to be a wonderful grandma. However, I think Lily may end up having to put her foot down about how much Pippa tries to take over with the babies.

"Carla, come sit down and tell me about my son, Sebastian, I mean."

I glance at Lily, who has a huge grin splitting her face, as Pippa takes her seat in the recliner next to Lily's bed with her grandson in her arms. This allows Lily to feed Charlotte.

Perching on the end of the bed instead of the chair, I swing my leg—a nervous habit of mine—so I clamp my hand down on my thigh. I look up and realize that Pippa is indeed waiting for an answer.

"Um, I'm not too sure what you want to know." I bite my lip.

Pippa starts to chuckle. "Carla, please stop blushing. I'm not going to eat you, and I'm thrilled that you and Sebastian are finally together." She raises an eyebrow.

Lily bursts out laughing. "What Pippa wants to know is if Sebastian has proposed. She's been on pins and needles since he mentioned marriage yesterday, and not even her new grandchildren can take her mind off the words he spoke."

"He hasn't asked me... yet." I offer a wry grin. "He told me he wants to ask me, but he wants to plan something I'll never forget." I become serious and look at Pippa. "I love him. I've been falling for him since your wedding." I look at Lily. "It hurt not being able to be with him because everyone thought I was with Ramon. By the way, he's my best friend, along with Sebastian."

Pippa shakes her head. "I felt for Sebastian. I'm his mom, and I knew there was something going on between you two. I know you weren't together like you are now, but it hurt to watch him suffer. It was what he needed to get on the right track, but I'll always be his mom."

Lily finishes feeding Charlotte and puts herself back in her nightdress before offering Charlotte to me.

I love babies, and I usually like that I can give them back when they get cranky. Right now, though, Charlotte is asleep, so I have no qualms about cuddling her. That's how Sebastian finds us when he walks into the room with his brothers.

Sebastian

Watching Carla cuddle my niece stirred something inside me. She'd be a great mom, and I'm sure we'd enjoy getting her pregnant. It would just be the delivery nine months later that would freak me out. However, I'd love to see Carla with my child growing in her belly. Being able to watch her cuddle our child, as she did with Charlotte at the hospital, would be a miracle. A delightful miracle.

Sighing, I glance at the woman beside me, who isn't far from my thoughts. She's sleeping in the passenger seat as I drive us out of town to a piece of land I want her to see. I'm not surprised she's exhausted, considering yesterday's turmoil and last night's lovemaking. I'm just glad she has an appetite like mine.

Her eye is slightly bruised, as is her shoulder. Other than that, she's assured me she's fine and just wants to carry on as normal, which is easier said than done. We can move on, but I won't forget that I almost lost her because of him. He needs to pay.

I slow down as the land I want to show Carla comes into view on our right. It's about a ten-minute drive from my parents' ranch, located on the outskirts of McKenzie Land. On our twenty-fifth birthdays, each of us received an acre of land spread around my family's ranch house. Not too close, but close enough.

Up until now, it's been the place I go to think. It's the one place in the world that is truly mine. It's land that I don't have to negotiate or write a contract for.

As I sit and look around now, I see that the light snowfall we've recently had has melted due to the warm weather we've been lucky enough to have. Carla starts to stir in her seat, stretching her arms up and arching her back.

"Where are we?"

I climb out of the SUV, run around to open the door, and hold my hand out to her. "I want to show you something. Hop out." I pull her out and give her a hug before letting her go to get the blanket from the back of the car.

I take her hand, and she raises an eyebrow in question. I just smile and continue walking through the trees to the clearing.

"Wow, Sebastian, this is gorgeous. Where are we?" she asks, breaking free and spinning in a circle.

God, I love this woman.

"We're standing in the backyard of our home."

She stops spinning and gives me a quizzical look, but then she gets it.

"You're building a house here?"

I walk toward her, grinning. "No, baby. We're building a house here— You and me. I own this land, which is part of my parents' property, so we're going to build a life here."

I kiss her lips, take her hand, and walk toward where I've planned our kitchen to be. It's the heart of a home, as my mom was forever telling us.

Feeling sick, I toss the blanket down before dropping to one knee.

Carla freezes, not taking her eyes off mine, as I hold out the engagement ring I've had since I was twenty-two, when my grandmother passed away.

"I'm not good at speeches, Carla, but I want you to know that I love you. I fell in love with you when I thought you belonged to my brother." I give her a nervous smile. "I'll always be true to you. No matter where I travel for work, if you can't come with me, I'll always come home to you and our children. Carla, will you marry me?"

Crying, Carla drops to her knees, throws her arms around me, and kisses my face. This causes me to lose my balance, and we fall over with her on top of me.

She holds out her hand, and I slide the ring onto her finger. I kiss her finger. We're officially engaged! I should be terrified, but I'm not. In fact, I can't wait to have her as my wife.

"I'll never forget today. I couldn't have imagined a more romantic proposal than on the grounds of our future home." She kisses me gently and sweetly, and my dick hardens and my blood boils.

Carla sits up, straddling me. "Make love to me, Sebastian. Right here. Right now." She shimmies down my legs, kneels between them, unfastens my belt and buckle, and pulls down my zipper, freeing my cock.

Bending her gorgeous head, she licks me from base to tip, swirling her tongue around the head before taking me into her mouth and sucking.

I nearly bolt up from the ground in pleasure. She's damn good at suction. I take handfuls of her beautiful brown hair as she continues to suck and lick me, making my legs quiver and my balls pull up, feeling like they're about to explode.

I throw my head back, grit my teeth, and pull her mouth from me. "Seconds, babe," I groan.

She jumps up, shimmies out of her jeans and thong, and straddles me. She takes my quivering cock into her hand and lowers herself down. I groan as she moans.

"Babe, lift your top up. I need to see your breasts."

She doesn't need to be told twice and pushes her top above her breasts before unclasping her bra.

She's beautiful.

Arching her back slightly, she holds onto my thighs and starts to ride me. She's so wet that my cock glides easily in and out of her tight, wet cunt. I smile, thinking about how embarrassed she is by the word, but I know it turns her on to hear it.

Watching her ride me, I know I won't be able to last long. Her breasts bounce with momentum, and her nipples harden along with my dick.

Feeling lightning strike my balls, I reach up and pinch and roll her neglected nipples.

"Oh God, Sebastian. Help me. I'm close."

"Me too, baby."

I can't hold on anymore, and I grow longer and wider inside her. "I want to feel your pussy squeezing me."

"Sebastian! Ahhh!" she screams.

Shit. I grasp her hips, holding her tight against me, and shoot my load inside her. I coat her walls while she shudders and shakes on top of me, collapsing onto my chest.

With my arms tight around her, our breathing gradually evens out, and small aftershocks run through Carla. I whisper, "Cunt." She clenches around me.

I start to laugh. "Don't you dare tell me you don't like that word, because now I have evidence that it turns you on."

She groaned and buried her face in my neck.

"And you know. You never did answer my proposal."

She raises her head and frowns down at me. "Yes, I'll marry you. Yes, I'll have six babies." She grins as my eyes widen. "And yes, I will love nothing more than helping you build our home here. Which room did you propose to me in? Oh my God! Which room did we just have sex in?"

I pull her down to me, roaring with laughter. "We just christened the kitchen, babe, but I think we'll have to christen the kitchen counters eventually."

"Hmm, I like the sound of that."

19

Carla

I'M ENGAGED! I'M ENGAGED! MAYBE IF I SAY IT OFTEN enough, it will actually sink in. No matter how many times I look at my ring, I get butterflies. Last night, on the way back to the apartment, Sebastian told me that the ring belonged to his grandmother, which made it all the more special. All I wanted to do was shout it from the rafters!

Sebastian's idea was to avoid his mom for a week or so before officially telling her, but I doubt that will work.

It's so frustrating to constantly need a babysitter because of the bastard after me and, consequently, my brother. I hope Gary gets what he deserves because he needs to be stopped. I sigh and hold my hand up again to look at my ring. The sun catches it through the windows and sets the ruby alight.

If I thought Ramon would help, I'd drag him to the bridal boutique a couple of blocks over. But I've shopped with him once, and that was enough. He's my best friend—someone to talk to, drink with, and pick me up when I'm down—but when it comes to shopping, hell no.

I'm waiting for Ramon to finish his phone conversation before he takes me out for coffee. His idea of celebrating is Starbucks, which luckily is next door.

He was stunned at first when I came home wearing an engagement ring. Before congratulating us, he acted like my big brother and read the riot act to his own brother. I wasn't sure if they'd end up fighting.

Everything ended well, though, with Sebastian making love to me quietly in my bed because Ramon had stayed home since he needed his office first thing. But, heck, it's his apartment, and I sure don't want to kick him out.

Hearing Ramon's office door open, I peered over

the sofa on which I had been lying, waiting for him. "You done?"

"Yeah, I've worked up a thirst. You ready?" he asked, collecting his keys from the counter, waiting for me to join him.

I jumped up from the sofa, pulled on my sneakers, and followed him out of the apartment and into the elevator.

Sebastian had to go to the office today for a meeting he'd forgotten about, which was another reason Ramon slept in his own bed last night.

As we travel down in the elevator, Ramon takes my hand and plays with my ring. "So, you're really going to be my sister," he grinned. "You'll never have to worry about Sebastian, Carla. I know he's no saint, but he said he'd stop when he met the woman he wanted to give the ring to. He's done well." He kisses my hand and pulls me out when the elevator doors open.

"Do you want your vanilla latte?"

I look up at the menu as he pushes open the door to Starbucks. It's a silly habit, doing this when I always end up with the latte. "Yeah."

Ramon chuckles and goes to place our order while I sit on one of the sofas by the window. This Starbucks is larger than the other one, which is purely a takeout place in the shopping district.

"Here you go." Ramon puts my drink on the table and sits down opposite me, trying to ignore the stares he's getting from three girls in the far corner.

I take a sip of my latte and hide my grin, finding him amusing. "Do you know them?" I can't hold back my laughter anymore, so I put my drink down before it sloshes everywhere. "Ramon," I tease, "they probably think you're cute."

He really is blushing. I never thought Ramon was the blushing type. He always seems so self-assured, so this is sweet. Not that I'd tell him, though.

Ramon sits forward on the sofa, resting his elbows on the table, and finally meets my gaze.

"I miss your brother, Carla. It's like he took a piece of me with him when he left."

This man isn't missing my brother as a friend. He's missing him because he's in love with him. Reaching out, I take Ramon's hands in mine. "Are you keeping anything from me? About why he left?" I kiss his knuckles.

He shakes his head. "No, I told you everything. We argued the week before, but everything was back to normal by the time he disappeared. Carla, the detective I hired to look for him, has followed a lead down to Florida."

I freeze, then release his hands and sit back. My heart pounds with anxiety at the thought that my brother might be in Florida. What's down there? Or who?

"Do you know if he has any friends down there? Someone he might have met through work when he was in Canada?"

I shake my head and turn to look out the window, trying to think. My brother had a few friends in Canada, but I don't remember him mentioning where they were from. All these thoughts running rampant in my head make my head spin and make me want to cry.

"If he does, then he's never said." I take another sip of my latte before looking out the window, expecting to see my brother walk back into Ramon's building. I swipe a tear away and am about to turn back when I feel as though I'm being watched.

I sit up straighter on the sofa and start really looking. I take notice of the stationery cars, the women walking past, ushering children along beside them or in strollers, and the men in business suits or more casual clothes. Then I spot him.

"Carla, what is it?"

He can't be there. Not with so many people around. Surely not.

Ramon starts to stand up, and I do too. He wraps his arm around my waist. "Carla, snap out of it and talk to me."

Swallowing, I turn to face him. "I think I saw Gary," I whisper.

He turns his head so quickly to look out the window that I'm surprised he doesn't get whiplash.

"Shit. Are you sure?" He grips both my arms and stands so close.

"I'm sure. It's a face I wish I could forget, but I doubt I ever will."

Ramon starts pulling me toward the exit. "We need to go back upstairs. Then, I'll ask security to show me the outside footage to see if he climbed into a car or if someone else was with him." He presses the elevator call button. "Hopefully, it will show what he was doing before you saw him."

I can't stop shaking, and Ramon notices. He pulls me straight into his body and holds me tight. "He won't get to you this time, Carla. I promise." He kisses my head. "I'll call Sebastian soon, okay? He's in a meeting right now, but when he's done, we'll tell him.

Hopefully, he won't be too mad at me for not telling him sooner."

"It's okay." I say, but I want to call him just to hear his voice and have him here with me, his arms wrapped around me.

Sebastian

Jacky is really pissing me off. Before the meeting, I'd been in the office for about twenty minutes, and Jacky spent almost all of that time parading back and forth through my office door.

I've told her on more than one occasion that I wasn't interested, but she was either dense or ignorant. While I dictated a couple of letters for her to type up, she sat across from me, crossing and uncrossing her legs and showing me more than I needed to see.

During the meeting, she sat at the opposite end of the conference table, taking notes. Every time I glanced in her direction, she wrapped her tongue around her pencil and licked it.

What I can't figure out is why she's doing this. Jacky is an attractive woman with the assets to match. She also has a good brain when she decides to use it. The fact that she won't leave me alone just doesn't make sense.

Crap! I hear my door open again and watch her saunter across my office before sitting in the visitor's chair across from me.

"Why do you keep ignoring my text messages?" Jacky flicked the hair on her chest behind her, giving me a view of her cleavage, which was practically hanging out of her dress.

I run my fingers through my hair and realize that I'm going to have to be more direct, regardless of whether I hurt her feelings. If she doesn't like it, I'll have to transfer her to a different department or fire her, which will be a last resort.

"I haven't replied to your text messages because there's nothing to say. I took you out once, thanks to my brother." I sit back in my seat and watch her, wondering what she's thinking—probably that I'm a jerk. Damn, Ruben. "I'm in love with someone else, so please stop texting me, Jacky. There will never be anything more than work between us." I sigh. "We've had this conversation before and I thought you understood."

She still doesn't say anything, so I go on, "I'm sorry if I led you on. That wasn't my intention. But we need to get back on track. So no more flirting with me. Just work. Okay?"

She stands and slowly stalks toward me. She rests her hands on my desk before leaning forward. "You're an ass." She straightens up and turns to leave. "But I can still work for you. I'm a professional, if nothing else."

My eyes widen at her words. I expected more of a tongue-lashing, but she spoke too calmly. I pray it isn't the calm before the storm.

She slams the door behind her, and I sag in relief. After a couple of minutes, I calm down and pick up my cell phone to speed dial Carla, who answers right away.

"Hey, babe. Did you get your latte with Ramon?" She loves Starbucks lattes, and if she hadn't talked me into going back to bed this morning, I would have had time before my meeting to stop by and get her one. As it was, she had to wait for Ramon.

"I did. How was your meeting?" She sounds odd.

"My meeting was fine. Is everything okay? You don't sound like yourself." I spin around in my chair and look at the Lexington skyline. I often caught my brother, Michael, doing this when I called in unannounced.

"I think I'm coming down with a cold. I'm not too bad, really, just a bit sniffly."

She actually sounds upset. "Babe, are you sure everything is okay? I was going to go to my apartment to get more clothes to stay with you, but I can come straight there."

"Sebastian, I promise I really am okay. I'd rather you go get some more clothes so you can stay here with me."

"Okay, I'll do that. Is Ramon there for a quick word?" With the phone between my shoulder and neck, I start packing my bag so I can leave while talking. The sooner I get to my apartment, the sooner I can be with my girlfriend.

We're planning on announcing our engagement to the family tonight, and I'm nervous about it. What I haven't told my brothers is that I can't wait to see who Mom chooses as her next victim of the wedding bug. Two of my brothers are definitely upset about women, so it's going to be fun to sit back and see who falls next.

"Carla, are you still there, babe?"

"Yeah, sorry. Ramon's on his phone right now. Do you want me to get him to call you back?" She sounds distracted now. Well, at least that's better than being upset.

"No, it's okay. I'll catch up with him later. I'm just about to get in the elevator, so I'll see you soon. Remember, I love you."

She chuckles. "I love you, too. Now hurry home so I can show you how much."

As soon as I step into my apartment, I drop my bag on the floor by the hall table, toss my keys into the tray I keep there, and yank my tie off. I hate those things, which is why I've spent years working from the site offices of our ongoing developments, but thanks to Michael, I have to put up with this for a while longer. Honestly, I don't begrudge him the time he's spending with Lily and the babies. I mean, God knows he deserves it after everything he went through before meeting his wife.

As I walk to my bedroom, I pull out a bag and

start shoving clean underwear in, followed by a couple of pairs of jeans and shirts. I grab my Chucks from the closet floor, tossing them on the bed beside the bag, and take out another suit, shirt, and tie in case I need to go to the office before next week.

With Jacky's help, I've rescheduled most of my meetings, except for three. Michael has offered to do those as long as someone is at the house to look after Lily and the babies.

As I try to think if I've missed anything, I realize I need my razor and a few other things from the bathroom. Once I get in there, though, I decide to take a quick shower. I might as well go back to my woman feeling refreshed.

I strip in the bedroom, leaving my clothes on the bed, and turn to head back into the bathroom when my doorbell rings.

Fuck! Who the hell has gotten past security?

I quickly grab a towel and wrap it around my waist. I hold it in place and look through the security peephole. I see Jacky standing on the other side. What the hell?

Without thinking, I pull the door open, then remember that I'm only wearing a towel.

"You're gorgeous." She steps closer, places a bright

red fingernail on my chest, and moves it south before I come to my senses.

"Jacky, what the hell are you doing here?" I practically growl at her, unable to hold my temper in check, and knock her hand away.

"Well, really. What did you expect me to do when you answered the door wearing only a towel?"

"That doesn't answer the question as to why you're here instead of the office."

"You wanted these letters to go out today, but you left before signing them." She stands in front of me, smiling as if to say, "You're an asshole."

"Shit. Give me ten minutes to shower and get dressed. Go wait through there."

Hell. There's no way I'm signing all ten letters while wearing only a towel.

I dash back into the bedroom, think twice, and lock the door because Jacky is someone I don't trust.

Stepping under the hot stream of water, which feels good pounding down on my tense shoulders and neck, I reach for the soap to make it a quick shower.

20

Carla

"Carla, I don't like the idea of you walking into Sebastian's building alone." Ramon dragged his hands through his hair. "You know the security there is terrible. The guard is more interested in his porn magazines than in making sure the building is safe."

I walked over to him, wrapped my arms around his waist, and leaned in for a hug. Ramon finally accepted it by hugging me back.

"I'm only thinking about you. You know that, right?" He kisses the top of my head.

"I know, but there will be more people outside

than here, so I should be okay. Please, Ramon. I really want to surprise him."

He's so cute right now. I just want to keep hugging him. "Please—"

He throws his head back. "Shit. Sebastian is going to kill me."

"No, he won't. I won't let him."

"Fuck. Get whatever you need, and let's go."

"Yes." I jumped up, kissed him, and ran to my room for my bag and jacket.

Yeah, I know I'm acting like a child, but I can't help myself. I only saw Sebastian this morning, but I can't wait to see him again at his place.

In my room, I quickly change out of my yoga pants and shirt before running to my closet for my red wrap dress and matching heels. I throw them onto the bed while stepping into the bathroom.

Sebastian has a fondness for my cherry-scented body lotion. With that in mind, I slather it all over, then rinse my hands in the sink.

Back in the bedroom, I quickly put on my clothes before slipping my feet into the shoes. Standing back, I look into the full-length mirror on my closet door and decide that I look hot. Sebastian will drool.

"Carla, what are you doing in there?" Ramon shouts right outside my door.

"Changing." When I open the door, Ramon's mouth drops open when he sees me.

He starts to laugh. "In that outfit, I don't think you'll make it to his bedroom."

"Ha ha. Very funny." I walk toward the apartment door and turn back to him. "I just want to make one stop on our way."

Hearing Ramon groan at the idea of stopping, I can't hold back my grin. When he sees the shop I want to stop at, he's going to be speechless.

WALKING THROUGH SEBASTIAN'S APARTMENT BUILDING lobby makes me feel apprehensive. What if he doesn't want me here? He gave me a key card and security code for the elevator and his apartment, but he always said the security is laughable and that I should stay away. Is that the only reason? I've never had reason to doubt him since we've been together, so why am I now?

He'll probably flip out when he finds me alone at his apartment.

With butterflies in my stomach, I enter the elevator and press the button for the ninth floor. The security guard doesn't look up from his paperback.

I peek inside my bag at my purchase and wonder how Sebastian will feel about it. I made Ramon pull over outside one of my favorite shops to buy a deep purple feather boa. Seeing the feathers sticking to him at Kenza, when Cat Woman and Poison Ivy accosted him on the dance floor, gave me a wicked idea. Ramon blushed and told me he didn't want to know what I'd bought. Of course, I teased him with the feathers but kept the black rabbit hidden.

Stepping out of the elevator, I quickly shove the bag of loot into my messenger bag and knock on Sebastian's apartment door. I knew I had the key, but it felt kind of awkward to use it when I hadn't before.

When no one answers, I knock again, and just then, I hear someone unlock the door. The door opens, leaving me speechless.

All the words desert me, and I feel my blood rushing through my head. My heart sinks as I watch Jacky, wrapped in a towel, stare back at me.

"Hurry up and say something. He's waiting in the shower." She stands with one hand on her hip and the other still holding the door open.

"Tell Sebastian I hope he'll be very happy." My voice breaks as I whirl around and run back inside the elevator. Thank God the doors are still open!

Sebastian

The water has cooled, so I turn off the shower, step out, and grab a large towel to dry off with. I hope Jacky has gotten bored and left. I tried to stay in the shower as long as possible, but I have a feeling she's still out there in my apartment.

Looking at my jaw, I decide to shave quickly. Not only will it delay the inevitable, but I'll also be smooth for when I get between my woman's legs.

My woman. I like the sound of that, and it's the first time I've ever called anyone "my woman." One look from her makes my heart flutter and my cock harden. She has a way of looking at me that says I'm all she sees. There isn't anything more powerful than having that look on her face.

I've seen the look on my brothers' faces when she gives me that come-hither look. They know I'm completely pussy-whipped, and I don't give a damn. I'd be pussy-whipped every fucking day if it meant she was my woman.

Leaving the bathroom, I shove my legs into my shorts before grabbing a pair of jeans, which I quickly pull on. Then, I slip my feet into my Converse.

I can't avoid Jacky anymore. I know I'm also going to have to transfer her to a different department. I unlock my bedroom door and walk out, but I stop dead in my tracks when I see Jacky standing near my front door with my gym towel wrapped around her.

What the fuck!

"Jacky?"

She spins around with a guilty look on her face but keeps looking toward the door.

"Why are you wrapped in my gym towel?" I glance toward the open bag under the hall table. "Where are your clothes?" I rake my fingers through my hair, starting to get a really bad feeling about all this.

"I—um—" She starts to unwrap the towel, and

thank God, her clothes are still on. What is she playing at?

I watch her pull the straps of her dress back up her arms and slide her skirt down her legs slightly.

"There was someone here. I wanted them to think we were together and about to shower," she says, turning on the waterworks. "Sebastian, I'm really sorry. I knew it was wrong as soon as she ran."

I freeze. She— "Who, Jacky?" I growl. "Who?"

She starts to back up at my anger. "Ramon's girl. I'm so sorry."

I walk toward her, grab her purse from the hall table, and shove it at her. Then, I open the door and shove her outside. "I'm arranging a transfer for you as of tomorrow. Personnel will be in touch with your new responsibilities."

"Sebastian, I'm sorry. Let me talk to her. Let me make this right," she whines.

My patience has flown the coup, so I slam the door in her face.

I race to my bedroom and grab a shirt, which I have the habit of going without around my apartment. Once I put it on, I reach for my phone to call Ramon and find out where he is and why Carla was here alone. I presume she was alone because my brother wouldn't let her leave. He would have demanded an explanation from me.

"Where's Carla?" I don't even let him say anything before shouting down the phone.

"What do you mean where's Carla? I dropped her off at your place about ten minutes ago. Are you telling me she never made it up to you?"

"She made it." I lean against the kitchen counter to catch my breath. "I was in the shower, and Jacky answered the door. She made it look like she was about to join me in the shower. I have no idea what was said, but I guess she took one look at her in my gym towel and fled."

"What the hell was Jacky doing in your apartment?"

"Fuck. I left the office before signing some letters. She brought them here for me to sign so she could mail them. I wasn't going to sign them in a towel, so I locked my room and quickly showered. I closed my eyes and squeezed the bridge of my nose with my thumb and finger. "When I came out, I found Jacky standing in my gym towel, having just answered the door. She told me what she'd done, so I kicked her out. I need to get personnel to move her elsewhere.

Shit. I need to leave and go after Carla. She's going to think all sorts of things. I'll call you when I find her."

I shove my cell into my back pocket and collect my keys from the dish by the door. As I opened the front door, I came face-to-face with a gun being held by—I presumed—Gary.

"Back up nice and slow." He waves the gun in front of me while following me back into my apartment.

Carla

I RUN FROM SEBASTIAN'S APARTMENT TO THE elevators and constantly press the button for the ground floor. Finally, the doors lock me inside. I slump to the floor, letting the tears flow.

They continue all the way down to the lobby, where I pull myself up off the floor. I root around in my bag for tissues to stop the tears, but they keep coming.

My dash out of the building prompts the security guard to pull his nose out of his paperback, but I ignore him and push through the doors onto the street.

Not knowing which way to turn, I head right toward the busy part of downtown, knowing I'll be safer there, although what I really want is to be alone and wallow in my misery.

I know Jacky has a thing for anyone named McKenzie, but I always thought Sebastian wasn't interested in her. I know he took her out once, but he convinced me that his brother was responsible for the groping session outside his building that I witnessed and that he wasn't involved. Had he been telling me the truth? Ramon thought so.

"Hey, get back," someone shouts, nearly yanking my arm from its socket.

I turn around to tell the person off, but he points forward just as an eighteen-wheeler flies past.

He saved me from getting killed. I was so preoccupied that I hadn't been watching where I was going and had stepped out into the road.

"Thank you," I whisper, turning and pushing through the people waiting to cross. I realize I'm outside "La Brioche," a French bakery I like. Or rather, I like the almond croissants they make.

Mopping my tears up again, I try to pull myself together—at least long enough to order a latte and a croissant—because I think it would be safer if I sat for a while before walking in front of another moving vehicle.

After ordering the treats, but knowing my stomach won't cooperate, I take a seat in the corner to hide my face.

I sip my latte and ignore the croissant for now, knowing my stomach would revolt if I ate anything. My tears keep flowing as I try to figure out what to do. Gary is still out there, so the last thing I need is to go out alone because he will find me.

Sniffling into my coffee, I can't shake the feeling that something isn't right. Sebastian has done nothing but show me how much he loves me, so would he really hurt me like this? I also heard the shower running behind a closed door, and, come to think of it, I noticed a stack of papers on his hall table, along with Jacky's purse. Had she gone to Sebastian's apartment to get his signature and found him in the shower?

Why the hell did I run? I'm an idiot. I don't usually run from confrontations unless they involve Gary. So why did I run from this one? Stupid. Stupid. Stupid.

Drying my tears, I wrapped the croissant in a napkin and shoved it in my bag with the loot I'd forgotten about before walking out of the bakery.

I dash back down the street toward Sebastian's apartment. I'd be lying if I said I'm not apprehensive about what I'll find. I need to know what's going on because something's telling me to give him a chance and let him explain.

I hear my cell phone ringing in my bag and pull it out, looking at the screen—*Ramon*.

"Hey." I'm standing outside Sebastian's building because he's told me that there's no cell coverage in the lobby or elevators.

"She set you up, Carla. Where are you?"

I can hear the stress in his voice, but I can't form a coherent response.

"Carla. Dammit! Gary is still out there. You shouldn't be walking around alone, no matter what you think Sebastian is doing. You should have called me. I would have come and picked you up and beat my brother up for being a jerk."

"I'm sorry. I really wasn't thinking, and I've realized that it might not have looked the way it seemed. That's why I came back to his apartment. In fact, I'm standing outside right now."

I could hear his sigh of relief over the phone. "I'm on my way, so let him know I should be there in about ten minutes, okay?"

"Yeah." We hang up as I push through the doors and notice that the security guard has disappeared.

I press the call button for the elevator and glance around again, but there's still no sign of the guard. I shrug and step inside, watching the doors close, wondering what to say to Sebastian. I should have trusted him, but he shouldn't have been showering with "her" in his apartment.

If she won't leave him alone, she's going to have to deal with me in the future because he's mine. Right now, I'm pissed at myself for running instead of fighting back. I was just too shocked at the time to think straight.

As I walk out of the elevator toward Sebastian's apartment, I freeze when I hear glass breaking inside. Then, I hear shouting. Gary.

Without thinking, I put the key in the lock, quietly make my way inside, and leave the door partially open for Ramon, hoping he gets here quickly.

"Stop pissing me off! I'm not afraid to use this gun." I've used it before, but until my ex-girlfriend gets here, you're safe. I want her to watch you suffer until she tells me where her brother is."

Oh God.

"She doesn't know where her brother is, you fucker."

Gary roars, and then I hear something else break.

With my shoes left at the door, I slide along the wall closer to the living room. I'm not really sure what I'm going to do, but I won't let him lay a finger on Sebastian.

Sebastian

This bastard is going down the minute I get the chance. Not just for what he did to Carla, but because he needs to be stopped. We can't spend the rest of our lives looking over our shoulders for him.

"Why?" I ask, trying to control my anger.

He continues to watch me as though I haven't said a word.

"Why are you doing this? What has Carla ever done to you? Other than trust you?"

"I know you're sleeping with her. She's good, isn't she?" He says this with a smirk, obviously trying to piss me off.

I'm seriously going to kill this fucker. My temper has already reached its limit.

Gary stands and slowly walks toward me, not moving the gun from my face.

I clench my jaw and ball my hands into fists as he stands within a few feet of me.

"She told her brother about my drug habit. Then, he told his cop friend. How convenient that Noah's dropped off the face of the earth now, isn't it?"

He hits me on the side of the head with the butt of the gun, knocking me across the sofa.

When I grab my head, my hand comes away covered in blood. The pain is incredible, and I'm struggling to stay focused. After blinking a few times, my vision still wavers. My heart nearly jumps out of my chest when I spot Carla peeking around the corner leading to the hall.

I need to sit up straighter so he won't lose his focus on me. He can't know she's there. Or is this the distraction I need to attack?

Finally, I pull myself together without taking my eyes off him. I pull my shirt free and use it to try to stop the bleeding from my head. Breathing through the nausea, I prepare to attack because the minute he realizes I'm distracted, he'll turn. It's human nature.

Keeping my eyes on him, I glance to his right and see Carla again. But fuck, he doesn't react.

Gary steps further away from me. "So she's arrived," he smirks. "Unless you want me to shoot him, I suggest you get your sweet little ass in here."

"Carla, run!" I roar as Gary loses it and comes at me. This is the opportunity I've been waiting for. He keeps the gun pointed at me, but as he goes to hit me, I jump up from the sofa and take him down.

I shout, "Carla, get out of here!"

I grab his wrist, the one holding the gun. As we struggle with the gun, it goes off, and all I can hear is Carla screaming.

"Carla, are you hurt?"

Gary is still struggling underneath me. I need to subdue him so I can go to Carla. I feel sick with fright, especially now that she's stopped screaming.

"Carla?"

Fuck.

Gary finally loses his grip on the gun. I manage to send it across the floor before I start punching him. Even when he stops moving, I keep going. I can't stop. He hurt my woman. He might have shot her.

This thought finally stops me, and I realize I need

to get to her and make sure she's okay. Then, I hear Ramon talking to someone.

I look toward the entrance to the living room and see Carla kneeling on the floor while Ramon checks her out. He moves toward me but stops at the gun and reaches for it.

"Don't touch the gun," I say, trying to get to my feet. "Evidence."

He dashes over to help me the rest of the way up. After looking at the man on the floor, he looks at me and raises his eyebrow. "You need to get that bleeding stopped."

"Soon." I'm overwhelmed by the need to get to Carla.

Seeing her standing against the wall reassures me that she isn't as badly hurt as I originally thought.

"The cops are on their way. Are you okay?" Ramon asks, but I push him away.

I stagger toward Carla, my head throbbing and my knees feeling as though they're about to give way. Blood is still trickling down my face from the wound on my head, and I try to swipe it away, but more follows.

"Sebastian—"

"Stay where you are," I quickly shout. "There's glass everywhere, and you're not wearing shoes."

When I reach her, I crush her in my arms, holding her as tightly as I can. "Please tell me you weren't hit?"

She shakes her head and wraps herself around me just as tightly before bursting into tears.

"I'm sorry," she says, her voice muffled by my chest. "I should have trusted you. I just saw her and didn't stop to think until I nearly stepped in front of an eighteen-wheeler."

What the fuck?

"Explain. Eighteen-wheeler?" I took hold of her face, made her look at me, and used my thumbs to try to stop her tears.

"It doesn't matter. I'm okay, but you're not." She takes my hand and leads me to my bedroom, but Ramon stops us on the way.

"Um, you two planning on leaving me alone with the bad guy?" he smirks.

"He's out of it." I clasp his shoulder and apply slight pressure to let him know I'm fine.

The bedroom door is already open, so we enter. I sit on the edge of the bed, and Carla pushes me down. I watch her walk into the bathroom and retrieve the medical kit I pointed to.

"You don't have much in here." She roots through it, hiding her face from me. "Carla, come here." She shakes her head and ignores my outstretched hand. "I love you, Carla, and only you. Please look at me."

Slowly lifting her head, she meets my eyes, looking heartbroken.

"Oh, baby." I stand up a little and reach over, catching her wrist in my hand before pulling her down onto my lap. "I'm okay. I'm a bit dizzy, but I'm fine. I almost freaked out when I saw you standing in the hall." I lean in, resting my forehead against hers, until I remember the blood. "Can you put a Band-Aid on so we can go back to Ramon's? I'm not letting you go all night."

"Okay."

She reaches for the medical kit again and places it on the bed beside me. I root through it and pass her the antiseptic wipes. She uses them to clean me up. Yeah, it stings like a motherfucker.

"Nearly finished. It's still bleeding a bit. You might need stitches."

"Hell no." I see her startled expression. "I mean, I'll survive with you nursing me." I grin. There's no way I'm admitting that I'm scared of needles.

"Hmmm." She places strips over the cut and starts tidying up.

"What does 'hmm' mean?" I reach for a clean shirt and pull it over my head, feeling my muscles ache. I was tense, and it had been a long time since I took someone down, except for one of my brothers. That would be an easy move compared to what had to happen in there.

"Are you scared of needles?" She bursts out laughing.

"Of course not."

Ramon gives his two cents as he walks into the bedroom.

"Did you want anything in particular?"

"Thanks would be nice. The cops are here. They took him away, but they want to talk to you both." Ramon informs us on his way back to the living room.

"Shit." I sit back on the bed and look at Carla. "I just wanted to take you away from here and explain things properly about Jacky."

"Shush." She covers my mouth with her fingers. "I know all about Jacky. I realized something was off during my earlier visit, so I turned around and headed back here. Then, Ramon called me and explained everything. I should have trusted you from the beginning. I'm sorry."

I watch a lone tear trickle down her face before answering, "Baby, none of today is your fault. When Jacky arrived, I was only wearing a towel, so I left her in the hallway while I showered. I locked the bedroom door, not trusting her. I wasn't gone long, but I did try to put off having to face her. When I opened the door, she was wrapped in my gym towel. Her dress was underneath."

She nodded her head, looking sad. "I know you weren't being unfaithful. I didn't think, and by the time I did, Gary was already here. I'm so glad I came back."

I wrapped my arms around her waist and buried my face in her stomach, inhaling her scent. She always smells delicious, like a light, flowery fragrance. It's something I can't get enough of.

"Let's forget about it. What matters is that we're together and that Gary is locked away—hopefully for a long time. Let's get the statements over with so we can leave."

22

Carla

THE SHOWER BEATS DOWN ON ME, BUT I CAN ONLY SEE Sebastian at his apartment, getting hit in the head with the butt of Gary's gun. Tears flow with the water as I can't help but imagine what would have happened if I hadn't come back. What if Ramon hadn't returned when he did?

I sink to the shower floor as wracking sobs take hold of me. Curling into the fetal position, I let the tears flow. I'm crying for my missing brother, not knowing where he is. I'm crying because I no longer have any family. I'm crying for the beating I took, for how scared and in pain I was. Most of all, I'm crying because I nearly lost Sebastian.

"Oh God, babe." Sebastian opens the shower door and climbs in with me, fully clothed. "Shit, Carla." He pulls me into his arms and sits down on the shower floor, getting soaked while holding me tight as I cry all over him.

After what feels like hours but is probably only minutes, my tears start to dry up and I start to notice other things, like the fact that I'm sitting naked in the shower on top of a jeans-and-shirt-clad Sebastian.

Shaking off my misery, I move away from him and shake my head when he tries to keep me close. I kneel between his legs and rest my hands on his wet jeans-clad thighs. I slowly move my hands up to his zipper.

"What are you doing?"

Is he serious?

"What does it look like I'm doing?" I leave his groin, but not before noticing his rising bulge. I smirk, lean in, and kiss him.

I pour all my love for him into the kiss, which starts off gently and turns into so much more. Before I can catch my breath, he grabs my hips, pulls me onto his lap, and this time, I straddle him.

As my passion goes from zero to ten in seconds, I

slide my hands through his hair, gripping his head to keep him in place while I take what I need from him. Moaning into his mouth, I grind against him. He feels so damn good against me. Being naked while he's fully clothed is also a turn on, but probably not for long given how hard his dick is.

Breaking away from his mouth, I nibble my way along his jaw and down his neck to his collarbone. At the same time, I lift his shirt up and over his head and drop it on the shower floor beside us.

I kiss down his chest, spending more time on his nipples, then press tiny kisses along his ribs and the top of his V, which disappears into his jeans.

"Hmmm, I can't wait to get you out of these jeans. You're going to have to stand up."

He doesn't need to be asked twice and starts tugging the wet denim down his legs. I help him, although I think I'm more of a hindrance, especially when his engorged cock bursts free.

Forgetting about getting his jeans off, I take him in hand. God, he's beautiful, and he arouses me with his desire. I have an ache inside that only he can satisfy, and smoothing my hand over his foreskin as he leaks precum is damn hot.

He wobbles with his jeans around his ankles while

I swirl my tongue around the tip. I moan, tightening my hold on him and pulling him down to the base before sucking him into my mouth as far as he'll go.

"Fuck."

He's about to lose control—his legs quiver with need. It fills me with excitement. I know I can bring this powerful guy practically to his knees.

"Babe, let me go. My jeans," he groans. He slides his fingers into my hair, holding my head down with slight pressure, but it's nothing I can't pull away from if I need to. "You're so fucking hot down on your knees."

I suck and lick him deeper into my mouth, reaching behind him with my hands and scraping his butt with my nails.

He shivers and throws his head back. "You're damn good at that," he growls as the head of his penis touches the back of my throat.

I look up at him and finally meet his gaze as I bring him to ecstasy with one hand on his balls and the other between his legs. I suck him in, swallow, and moan. He curses as his semen shoots down my throat, all without breaking eye contact. I continue to suck him off, but he eventually moves my mouth away.

"No more." He collapses against the shower wall.

I crawl to his feet, untangle his legs from his jeans, stand up, and switch off the shower. I climb out and grab a couple of towels. I dry off and turn to pass one to Sebastian, who emerges weak in the knees.

There's nothing I can do, so I grin and start to laugh when he frowns, trying not to join in.

"Okay, I admit defeat. That was fucking awesome," he says, grabbing me around the waist. "Shit, I can't feel my legs."

I kiss his nose, break free, and run out of the bathroom. I take a running jump onto the bed with a smug smile on my face. I feel so damn tall, not to mention aroused as hell.

As Sebastian follows me out, he grabs my bag from the chair. "Ramon told me to check your bag for loot. Whatever that means."

I cringe, knowing damn well what he's going to find. I'm not embarrassed about the feather boa, but I am about the black rabbit. I'd planned on working my way up to using it on him.

Sebastian

What the hell? I look into Carla's shopping bag, but all I see is a rabbit. Ignoring the feather boa, I retrieve the "thing."

I hold it up and watch Carla squirm on the bed. "You want to try this out?" I raise an eyebrow.

"I bought this to use on you."

She snickers at my shock now. How does she plan on using this on me?

"I was planning on using it on you while I sucked you off."

This woman is going to kill me. I intend to go slow, but after hearing her, I'm not sure that's going to be possible. "Seriously?" I look down at my straining erection. Well, at least we agree on where it wants to go.

"Why are you laughing?"

I'm in trouble. She moves to the middle of the bed and opens her legs. She caresses herself, starting at her pussy and moving up to her breasts, which she's now playing with. Mesmerized, I slowly walk toward her as I watch her massage and pinch her nipples, which stand at attention alongside my cock.

She's watching me through her half-closed eyes. If

she can put on a show, then so can I. I drop the rabbit on the bed and reach between my legs. I stroke my balls before caressing the weeping tip. I take a firm hold of my length and move my hand back and forth, creating delicious, toe-curling friction.

Carla moves one hand from her nipples and slips it between her legs, parting her folds. She arches her back when she touches her clit, moaning.

Fuck. My balls are on fire.

Within seconds, I'm on top of her. I pin her wrists above her head, bringing us nose-to-nose. I try not to come as her channel clings to my dick.

"If anyone brings you to orgasm, it's going to be me. Not your fingers, no matter how hot it is to watch. No one but me." I grin. "Although, I'm all for playing with the rabbit."

She chuckles, and the flutters that run along my cock are caused by her muscles squeezing and relaxing.

"Wrap your legs around me."

As she does, I slide even deeper.

Breathing heavily, I try to curb the impulse to pound into her because my orgasm is hovering on the edge and feels damn good.

"I'm not going to come inside you."

She frowns in question.

"We need lubrication for your 'friend.'" It takes her a minute, but when she understands, her face splits into a huge grin.

"That sounds so fucking hot. Now shut up and fuck me."

Growling, I slam my lips against hers, sucking her tongue while she thrashes around underneath me.

"Move," she moans as I bite down on one of her nipples. I pull out almost completely before thrusting back in, over and over again.

She tries to break free from my grip on her hands, but it's too tight. Not enough to hurt her, but enough so she can't break free.

"Don't you dare come, Carla. You hear me? You're not going to come until Mr. Rabbit and I are inside you."

Fuck, I'm about to come too.

I quickly pull out and go up on my knees, taking my cock in my fist, and come all over her pussy. Jesus. Fuck.

"Oh God, babe. Hot damn."

I stroke her thighs as I try to even out my breathing because that was fucking hot.

"Sebastian, I need you."

Carla is lying gloriously naked with her thighs on either side of me. My come is between her legs, and she's desperate for her orgasm, which she's going to get real soon, provided I don't mess up.

Rubbing a finger through my semen on her pussy makes Carla moan and arch up into my hand. She wants me to move lower, so I do when she widens her legs. I rub my semen slowly between her thighs and along her ass, gently massaging it and slipping my finger easily between the tight, puckered hole.

I withdraw my finger, flip her onto her stomach, and raise her hips, positioning her so that her beautiful ass is staring up at me while she rests her face on the bed with her arms on either side.

I massage her cheeks before bending down to nibble each one as my finger slips inside her wet channel. After a few strokes, I withdraw my finger and insert it into her ass again. She moans deeply into the bed.

My finger has easy access now, sliding in and out of her. She's panting with arousal, her hands gripping the sheet beneath her.

I pick up the rabbit, switch it on, and press it against her clit, hearing Carla curse and moan. My cock is hard as hell again, raring to go. This time, I intend to come with her.

I move my finger away and keep the rabbit on the first setting. I place the tip at her entrance, then slide it all the way in, coating it in her wetness.

"Lubrication," I whisper into her ear. But as I withdraw, I change my mind. I decide the rabbit can stay in her channel because I want to be in her ass.

I put the rabbit to the side and take my cock in hand, sliding it along her folds. I grit my teeth against the pleasure while Carla writhes around, trying to get me inside her.

I take the rabbit, insert it back inside her, and leave it on the second setting while I insert one, then two, fingers into her ass.

"Oh God, Sebastian. That's so good. Don't stop."

Unable to take much more, I remove my fingers and start entering her ass with my dick, sliding in an inch at a time. I go really slow, not wanting to hurt her as I continue to fuck her ass.

To be honest, this may not be the first time I've done this, but it sure as hell is the first time it's felt so damn good.

She's taken all of me, and I have to fight the urge to move while she gets used to the invasion. If that weren't enough, I can feel the slight vibration from the rabbit through the thin wall separating us.

"Sebastian, I can't take much more. Please move," she whispers, catching her breath. I withdraw before entering her again.

I can't stop now. I reach between her legs and turn the rabbit up. I pump in and out of her ass. Back and forth. Back and forth.

Then she screams and clenches around me so tightly—tighter than ever before. My balls ache with pleasure as the best damn orgasm in history rips out of me.

My eyes roll back in my head as she continues to thrash around, grinding against me and gripping and releasing my cock.

Fuck me! I give a couple of shallow pumps with my semi-erect dick before slowly sliding out of her ass. Just as I do, she reaches between her legs and pulls the rabbit out.

I collapse onto the bed beside her and pull her into my arms.

"I can't move."

"Me either, babe. Me either."

"What time did Ramon say we're expected at your parents' place?"

"Mom changed it to tomorrow night after he convinced her that we're okay and just need to rest tonight."

Carla starts laughing against me, and pretty soon, I join in. There hasn't been any resting yet, although I think that might be about to change because I'm exhausted, and I think my fiancée is too.

23

Carla

SEBASTIAN HELPS ME OUT OF THE CAR, BUT I CAN'T stop thinking about the lovemaking we shared last night and again this morning. It was the hottest experience of my life thus far, and I doubt I'll ever forget it.

We're here at his parents' house to announce our engagement, which I'm sure Pippa already knows about. I'd be very surprised if she hasn't gotten the information from Ramon.

"Are you ready to do this?" Sebastian takes my hand and waits patiently for my answer.

"I love you and your family, Sebastian. Yes, I'm ready."

We open the door, and I pull a reluctant Sebastian with me. The minute we shut the door behind us, we're ambushed by his mom.

"I knew it. I knew he'd propose soon. Let me see how the ring looks on your finger." Pippa releases me from her hug and holds my hand up for everyone to see.

I look around the room at the smiling faces of Sebastian's dad, brothers, and Lily, as well as Lily's friend Sabrina, who doesn't actually look that good.

"Perfect," Pippa says. "Now, all I have to do is find wives for your three brothers," she tells Sebastian, who snickers when he looks at his brothers.

"I think Ramon should be next," Sebastian announces.

Ramon pauses mid-drink, looking like a deer in headlights. "I think Ruben will be next because he can't keep his eyes off—" he grumbles, getting elbowed in the side by Ruben.

"Children, that's enough. Let's move this into the living room," Elias chides.

One of the things I love about being around

Sebastian's family is the interaction between the brothers. They have a habit of teasing each other like children, which can be so funny—and dare I say it—cute.

Walking into the living room, I see Lily sitting beside her double stroller with her three-day-old twins inside. Of course, I just have to check to see if they're awake.

"Don't worry," Lily says, seeing my disappointment. "They'll be awake soon, and then the fun starts. You can help with that, since you're going to be their aunt. You might as well get used to having a baby around."

Grinning, I reply, "Oh, I'd like that." Then, my eyes widened when I realized what she had actually said. "Um, I won't need to get used to a baby anytime soon."

"We'll see," Lily smirks.

I'm just about to look back at the babies when I notice Sabrina walking through to the back with her jacket in hand. "What's going on with Sabrina?"

"I'm not too sure. I tried asking, and she nearly bit my head off. I think there's something going on with Lucien. When I asked him about it, he asked me to drop it." She shrugs her shoulders. "Personally, I think

he really likes her but doesn't feel ready for a relationship because of his scars. I know his scars go beyond
what can be seen. I just don't know how to help him."

Thinking about what Lily said makes me smile
because I have a feeling Lucien has bitten off more
than he can chew with Sabrina.

"Anyway, how are you feeling, Lily?" I ask as she
sits back down, looking a bit awkward.

She laughs. "Yeah, I guess you noticed I'm a bit
uncomfortable. I'm not too bad, really. Just a bit sore
down below. But it sure is worth it." She leans closer,
giving me a mischievous smile. "Michael promised to
kiss it better once the bleeding stops."

"I bet."

"Hey, babe." At the same time, Sebastian wraps his
arm around me and passes me a glass of champagne.
"What are you betting on?" He kisses my forehead.

"Um, nothing." I glance in Lily's direction. When
our eyes meet, she winks.

"I was telling Carla that Michael promised to kiss
all my aches away." Lily turns back to her babies while
Sebastian leads me toward his brothers.

"She was referring to between her legs. In case you
were wondering," I whispered into his ear.

"I seriously did not need that image in my head. Now play nice." His hand slips to my butt.

"No chance. Besides, I was actually thinking about your head between my legs."

We come to a stop beside Ramon and Ruben, who look as though they caught my last sentence. I feel a blush creeping up my neck as I look at them, wondering if they'll comment. I hope Sebastian will say something to diffuse my embarrassment. But as I look at him, he seems to be enjoying the attention. Men!

"Fuck me. It's been too long since I've been between a woman's thighs," Ruben comments. He soon turns to a frown when he looks at the side of me. "Mom."

Ramon snickers.

"Hmm, well, at least I don't have to worry about becoming an unexpected grandmother."

The brothers roar with laughter.

It always amazes me how Pippa only has to say a few words, and her grown sons blush. I love being here with them and can't wait to become a permanent part of the family. I guess that will happen fairly soon if Sebastian has his way. But for me, since I intend to be married only once, I want all the trimmings, plus the perfect dress.

I also want to be married here, in the home where Sebastian grew up.

We'll see.

EPILOGUE

Carla

NEARLY NINE MONTHS AGO, IT ALL STARTED AT THE McKenzie ranch. Who would have thought that I'd be engaged to the delicious guy I couldn't take my eyes off of? He's the same guy who's given me countless sleepless nights since then. And I don't just mean because I was stressed out about who he was with or what he was doing, if you know what I mean.

He is standing outside the marquee, holding alcohol and chatting with Ruben, who doesn't seem to be paying attention, his gaze fixed on Rosie. He is so obvious.

Finally giving up, Sebastian starts heading in my

direction, leaving his brother to chase after Rosie, who is on her way to the barn. It wouldn't surprise me if she were sneaking off for a five-minute break from Ruben's orders.

Today has been beautiful, with the baptism of Michael Elias Jr. and Charlotte Lily McKenzie. They are the first grandchildren for Pippa and Elias, who have been showing them off like proud parents. The babies are three months old today, and they've certainly grown. Not to mention, they have all four of their uncles wrapped around their little fingers.

"Hey, sexy lady." Sebastian saunters closer, wearing the panty-dropping smile he used on me the first time we met.

I pretend not to be affected and reply, "Sebastian, I'm a sure thing. You don't need to practice your pickup lines on me." Shit. Now he looks upset. "I'm only joking. You can use any line you want on me, and I promise I'll drop my panties by the end of the evening."

His grin can't get any wider. "Now, babe, that's the kind of answer I like to hear."

I wrap my arm around him, reach up, and first kiss his ear before whispering, "If I'm wearing any, that is."

Sebastian

"If you're wearing any, fuck, babe. Do you have any idea what those naughty words do to me?" I turn my body toward hers, letting her feel my erection, which happens the minute she opens her mouth.

"You need to behave, because I'm not sneaking off with you for a quickie at your parents' place." She rubs against me a couple of times before pulling me down onto the wicker sofa my parents have out here.

Once seated, she leans back and places her legs across my lap. "Coverage," she laughs, just as Ramon and Lucien join us.

"Has he been keeping you awake all night?" Lucien smirks.

"Maybe," she chuckles. "What about you two?"

Ramon grins, but Lucien looks reserved.

"What about us two?" Lucien asks. I catch him watching Sabrina chat animatedly with Ruben, their hands on each other's arms. This puts a frown on Lucien's face.

"A body to keep you warm at night."

My hands are working magic on her feet. If she purrs any louder, though, we're going to start getting some strange looks. I catch Ramon watching with a grin on his face.

"So, Ramon, do you have a warm body in your bed?" she persists.

Before he can answer, we hear raised voices at the side of the barn. Carla sits up and follows our gaze just in time to see Ruben grab Rosie as she walks away from him. He spins her around and kisses her—and I mean kisses her. If the hands in Ruben's hair are anything to go by, she doesn't seem to be complaining. Unfortunately, the show ends too soon when they both let go of each other. Rosie runs off toward the cars, while Ruben stands there, watching her go. I pray he follows her, but he doesn't. Stubborn idiot!

"I think you were right about Ruben being next. That's been a hell of a long time in coming," Carla observes.

"Hmm, but I'm more interested in the catalog you were looking through with Lily right now." The only thing I saw when Lily quickly took the catalog from Carla's hands was a scantily clad woman in a scrap of lace.

"What about it?" she asks, a blush working its way up her neck.

Oh, this is going to be good.

"It was a Victoria's Secret catalog, if you must know. I can't exactly go on my honeymoon wearing old stuff. My groom is going to expect me to wear sexy pieces of material that barely cover the goods."

"Fuck, I'm outta here."

"Chicken," I shout to Ramon's retreating back before turning my attention back to my girl. "You're killing me. You know that?"

She sits up and straddles me. She wraps her arms around my neck, wiggles around on my cock, and meets my eyes.

"You do the same to me."

I brush her hair from her forehead and kiss her nose. I kiss her cheeks before taking her lips. She tastes of chocolate and coffee.

"I think you should climb off me before we give the baptism guests more than they bargained for." She grinds against me. "Babe," I whisper, which is becoming more and more difficult. All I want to do is drag her off to a private place so I can get under the long dress she's wearing.

"Besides, just think, in one month, I'll be Mrs.

Carla McKenzie, so we'll be legal. Actually, it has a rather nice ring to it."

"Hmm, being legal, you mean, or Mrs. Sebastian McKenzie?"

She rolls her eyes and climbs off me, allowing me to stand and wrap her in my arms. "I love you, my soon-to-be wife."

She kisses me. "I love you, too, soon-to-be husband."

The End

MCKENZIE BROTHERS
HOLDINGS

DEAR READER

Thank you for reading *Playing with Fire,* and thank you for your reviews! It's really appreciated.

Subscribe with your email to be alerted about new releases, sales, and events.

http://lexibuchanan.net

INDECENT VILLAIN
A DARK MAFIA ROMANCE

My parents descended into the ground while I stood motionless and unresponsive to the penetrating darkness that was Tiberius Beckett.

He moved into my home and I realized that the man had two sides, and he showed me his true face. I liked him. He became my obsession, as I became his. Together, we did some bad things.

Do you want to know more about Tiberius Beckett? Then let me tell you about my indecent villain.

Available Now!

INDECENT VILLAIN SNEAK PEAK

Prologue

Kinsley

Fragile.

I feel like I'm going to fracture into a thousand pieces.

I stand silent and motionless beside my parents' graves, rain soaking me to the skin. The wind whistles around my body as I remain unresponsive to the penetrating darkness directed at me by Tiberius Beckett, my father's brother. The man stands tall in his dark suit, his piercing gaze seeming to search for something within me, as if he knows a secret I'm not even aware of. Despite the storm raging around us, his presence feels more unsettling than the howling wind.

My tears mix with the rain and flow down my cold cheeks. The priest speaks loudly and clearly, but his words blend as my mind refuses to comprehend them. I swallow hard as my mother's casket is lowered into the earth. Then that of my father follows. It is the end for them, and for me, too. Tiberius, at my father's request, has become my legal guardian. He doesn't want me, just as I do not want him. I tell myself I'll endure for the next two weeks until I turn eighteen. It's not long, but it feels like an eternity.

I pray that I survive the man with silver eyes.

But no one survives Tiberius Beckett.

Tiberius

Fragile.

Kinsley looks like the wind will blow her over any second. The girl does not trust me. She will. My fingers yearn to stretch across the space between us and take her in my arms. I am a hard man. But with Kinsley, my heart is fucking mush. She is my vulnerability. The girl has been in my head for a while now. It kills me to stand here and watch her suffer alone.

She is unaware of the danger she is in, just as she is unaware that my men are hidden around the cemetery to keep her safe. Me too. However, they know she is their priority. I can take care of myself, but

Kinsley cannot. She needs me, even if she doesn't realize it yet.

The rain falls harder as my brother and his wife are now in the ground. Other mourners and the priest take their leave, while Kinsley and I remain. I stare at her. Kinsley lifts her face, her eyes finding mine. I don't look away, and neither does she. We stand there in silence as the rain soaks us both. In that moment, I know that I will do whatever it takes to keep the defiant young woman safe, even if it means revealing my true feelings.

Chapter One

Three days after the funeral, the rain continues to fall. The gardens have turned into fields of mud, and even the long driveway has puddles. My grand home looks gothic surrounded by the dark clouds and rain, but in the sun, it is beautiful. I've always found the house to be too spacious for our small family. The house once bustled with numerous servants, but that was before my time and before my father's as well. Grandfather used to tell me about the garden parties his mother hosted when he was six. Sadly, not long after that, there was a war. He said most of the servants left and took up arms for their country—mostly the men, but some of the women did too, I guess.

Sighing, I consider my predicament. Tiberius is a strange man and has the power to unnerve me. I think back to my younger years but can't really put my finger on when I started to feel that way. Maybe it had more to do with my father being unsettled around his brother than anything else. I must have picked up on his unease and let it affect me. However, Tiberius does nothing to help dispel those feelings around him. I think he enjoys it. I'm not like my father, though. I won't let the man push me around. I may have been showing weakness since my parents died, but no more. I'm not a little moth who needs nurturing. I'm nearly eighteen years old but feel older.

If I'm honest with myself, there is a slither of happiness within me that I will no longer be held prisoner in my home. My parents were afraid of something in the months leading to their deaths and had kept me home with a private tutor. I don't miss the city, but I do miss going into town, even if it is only for a cup of coffee while I watch the world go by. It's better than being locked up inside the Lake House.

I press a hand to my stomach, trying to quell the bundle of nerves that suddenly rises as I watch a large black car appear through the trees along the driveway. The wheels kick up muddy water as Tiberius brings the beast to a stop close to the front entrance. Another car, this one silver and sleek, pulls in beside the black one. The man has arrived, along with my parents' attorney.

Tiberius climbs from the driver's side of the car, while another man emerges from the passenger seat. They exchange words.

The attorney, Mr. Arnold Fielding, exits his car and runs for the front door. Tiberius takes one step and seems to be frozen to the spot. His head suddenly turns, and his gray eyes lift and find mine. Stunned, I gasp, but I refuse to look away first. My heart thumps heavily behind my breastbone. How did he know I was watching, and from where? He snaps his attention back to his passenger, a man in jeans and a tee. Unnerved, I head into the bathroom and splash cold water onto my face. I pat it dry with a fluffy towel. The mirror before me reflects my drawn expression. Dark circles are prominent beneath my eyes, the color matching my long hair.

A knock on my bedroom door draws my attention. I swallow hard, knowing there will be no escaping the next hour or so. Today is the reading of the will, followed by lunch with Tiberius. I am overjoyed.

Another knock.

"One moment," I shout.

I slide my feet into the shoes I kicked off earlier and take one last glance in the mirror. The dark color of my midi dress does nothing for my washed-out look. I open the door and catch the impatient look on the housekeeper's face.

"About time," Martha snaps before briskly turning away.

I roll my eyes and inhale, holding my breath for a few seconds before slowly exhaling. It helps center me when I know I am about to face danger. That is what Tiberius Beckett is to me—the devil himself.

And there he is.

His dark-gray eyes follow me as I move down the staircase, his body remaining still like a predator. I refuse to let him see the nerves that threaten to break me in his presence. He is the kind of man who, if you give him an inch, he will take a mile.

I come to a stop at the end of the stairs and hesitate. My father's office will be used for the reading of the will, and the thought of being locked behind closed doors with Tiberius and the attorney makes me want to run. Of course, I do nothing of the sort. I am an Elliot. I can do anything.

At that moment, Mr. Fielding appears.

"My dear, Kinsley," he says as he moves, taking my cold hands into his much larger and warmer ones. "I am sorry for your loss. Come and take a seat." He leads me into the office and sits me in a Queen Anne chair in front of the large window. The choice of seating arrangement surprises me, as the meeting table would have sufficed. Nevertheless, I accept the small cup of coffee he places in my hands.

"Thank you for your condolences. It is a very difficult time," I acknowledge, trying to act the way my mother would want me to—like a lady instead of a rebel. I lean forward and place the cup on the coffee table.

"Mr. Beckett," Mr. Fielding calls, "please take a seat beside your ward."

I cringe. I do not want to be his ward, nor do I want him sitting beside me. From his hesitation, I gather he doesn't want to sit beside me either. He takes the seat opposite, which is even worse. He won't miss anything now.

Mr. Fielding clears his throat and shoots an impatient glance toward the evil man. "Let's get started, then." He unbuttons his blazer and sits, a sheaf of papers in his hand. "Kinsley, you are aware that you are now the ward of Tiberius Beckett, at your father's request."

"For two weeks. Yes, I am aware."

My gaze lifts to the man in question. His hard face shows nothing of what he is thinking. Those dark eyes of his rove over me in a way that causes my heart to pound. The sneer on his cruel lips sets me on edge. As we are, it is the first time I have been close to the man. He looks younger than I first thought. Early thirties to what I previously labeled as early forties. His thick black hair curls over his ears. High cheekbones are marked by a scar across one of them. His rugged features give him a dangerous air, but there is a fleeting hint of vulnerability in his eyes. Have I misread them? The way they narrow on me, I think not. He hates that I've seen it. Despite his intimidating presence, I feel a flicker of curiosity about the man who now holds power over me.

A throat clears, which forces my gaze away from Tiberius. Mr. Fielding clears his throat once more. "The last will and testament is rather brief, I am afraid." He looks at me over the rim of his glasses perched on the end of his thin nose. "Your father wasn't one for time-wasting."

"Get on with it," Tiberius growls as his tattooed hands clench his thighs.

"It is a joint will with your mother." Mr. Fielding clears his throat again, which is becoming annoying. "We hereby leave all our assets to our daughter, Kinsley Elliott. The house we also leave to our daughter—"

"What?" Tiberius questions in a quiet but deep voice as his attention snaps to the attorney. His eyes narrow. "He left the house to"—he turns and glares my way with hatred—"her?"

The papers shake in Mr. Fielding's trembling hands. "That is what he wrote."

"What is going on?" I ask, annoyed. Why would Tiberius be upset that my parents left our family home to me? It makes no sense. But then it makes no sense that I would be left as Tiberius's ward when the man had made my father nervous.

"You want to know the truth, little girl?" he sneers and stands. He shoves the coffee table out of the way and leans over me, his hands tightly gripping the arms of my chair. When he is so close that I can see silver mixed in with his dark-gray eyes, he says, "The house was supposed to be left to me. I had an agreement with your father." His eyes blaze with emotion. "I have your father's signature on the agreement between us."

I'm trying to concentrate as Tiberius is making a point, but all I can think about is the heady scent of his cologne. It seeps into my senses and gives me ideas I should not be having.

"You smell nice," I blurt.

His brows shoot up to his hairline as he tightens his jaw and takes his seat, his face on the lawyer. "The house is rightfully mine. I won't sit back and accept this," he scoffs. "Even in death, he's doing his upmost to fuck with me."

I place a trembling hand on my stomach while I fight to get my equilibrium back. His reaction confuses me. I don't want to draw attention to myself, but I must ask, "Why would you think you're entitled to this house?"

"Because," he grinds out, "the house belongs to the oldest living male relative. With Jude gone, that is now me. It's the way it has always been done."

"Why didn't I know about that?" I ask softly, feeling like my family betrayed me. "I don't understand my father. I have only ever seen you from a distance, but now I am your ward. Why?"

Tiberius frowns when his eyes land on me. "None of that matters now."

I force my gaze to the lawyer. "If Tiberius thought he was getting the house, then am I correct to assume my father made a previous will? What was in it?"

"That doesn't—"

"Tell her," Tiberius snaps.

Mr. Fielding takes a sip of the glass of water in front of him, and says, "In your father's previous will, he left the house to Tiberius Beckett and explained why. As Tiberius said, the eldest male descendant was to inherit the house."

"My father was Jude Elliott. How are you a Beckett?"

"That piece of paper in your hand will not stand up in court when I have my lawyer file an objection." The man totally ignores me and speaks to Mr. Fielding.

A headache brews behind my temples, and I want to leave the room. I feel sorry for Mr. Fielding, who has done nothing but read my parents' wishes. Tiberius reminds me of a bull ready to charge. His nostrils flare, and his large body tightens with suppressed anger. He is a tall man who obviously takes good care of himself. The muscle he possesses is unable to hide behind the clothes he wears.

I sense the tension in the room escalating as Tiberius's anger becomes palpable. I need to diffuse the situation before it escalates further. My hands feel sweaty and my mouth is dry, but I have to say something to calm Tiberius down.

"I don't want the house. He can have it." I rush the words out and bring the two men to silence. In truth, the house is the only home I've ever known, but I always planned to leave when I turned eighteen.

"What?" Tiberius shakes his head. "What did you say?"

I swallow hard, and say, "You can have the house." I turn my gaze to Mr. Fielding. "You can arrange that, right?"

"Actually"—the older man sighs—"nothing can be done until you turn twenty-one."

Tiberius releases a string of curse words, some of which raise my eyebrows in shock. As difficult as it is to ignore his strong presence, I turn away from him and give my full attention to Mr. Fielding. I need to concentrate.

"I'm assuming there is a clause about selling the house."

"It states that you must live in the house until you turn twenty-one, after which time, you can leave and pass on ownership. However, your father stipulated that ownership could only be passed to Tiberius Beckett."

"Let me get this straight. My father left me the house, yes?" He nods. "But I have to continue living here until I turn twenty-one, at which point he expects me to hand the house over to him." I point toward the beast of a man.

"That is correct."

"Why didn't he just leave the house to him in the first place? This doesn't make any sense." I get my unsteady legs under me and stand. "What about college? How will I go if I must live here?"

"That detail we will discuss at another time," Tiberius says, calm once more. He takes out a piece of gum and moves it between his fingers. Is he trying to quit smoking?

"My father was afraid of you." It takes courage, but I manage to hold his gaze. "Why would he make me your ward?"

"I'm the only one who would have you."

"That's not quite—"

"Mr. Fielding," snaps Tiberius. "Thank you for your time this morning. I will bring my niece into your office next week to sign the documents you have for her." He ushers the lawyer from the room.

My refusal to join Tiberius for lunch has garnered his anger once more. The man takes my arm and drags me into the formal dining room, where he pushes me into a chair beside the one at the head of the table, which he takes.

"You need to eat." His large hands tighten around his cutlery. "You've lost weight since the last time I saw you."

In truth, I am hungry. The food in front of me looks more appetizing than anything Martha has prepared since my parents died.

"Hmm," I mutter as I straighten in the chair and start to eat. Tiberius watches me with a calculated look on his face as he continues eating.

The food is pleasant, which puts me at ease and leads me to ask, "Will you be moving in?"

He nods.

"Good. At least we'll get something edible."

He pauses with a fork of beef near his lips. "Explain that comment." He places his knife and fork on the plate and sits back, his gaze unwavering.

"Since my parents died, the food hasn't been good." I sigh. "I'm not allowed in the kitchen to make my own, so it's no wonder that I've lost weight. I hate tuna, which Martha serves me on crackers for lunch daily."

"I shudder at the thought," he says. In his next breath, he shouts, "Martha!"

The woman who hates me comes dashing into the room. "Sir?"

My cheeks flush hotly, and I silently plead that he won't drop me in it with her. Tiberius narrows his eyes on my face, and his jaw twitches.

"I will be moving into the house later today, and I expect breakfast and dinner served in this room with my niece daily, unless otherwise stated. There will be no tuna and crackers." He pauses for a moment, holding her full attention. "There will also be no seafood put on the table. Ever."

Martha shoots me a look of hatred before she says, "Yes, sir."

"My niece is the owner of this house, which means she is your employer. If you value your position here, I suggest you treat her with respect. She needs to eat, not starve. Do I make myself clear?"

"Yes."

"Yes, what?"

"Yes, sir."

Tiberius snorts. "Go." He turns to me. "I have no clue what I am supposed to do with you."

"You could ignore me, and I will ignore you."

He grins, which surprises me. He has to be the most handsome man I've ever seen. "You're too pretty to be ignored, and I'm too big and loud." He frowns. "Others will be moving into the house with me. You need to stay out of their way." He points his fork in my direction. "They are dangerous men. I will only give you this warning once. You understand me?"

It's a good thing I've eaten all my food, as my appetite suddenly disappears. "I understand." My mind whirls, wondering who they are and why he has dangerous men living with him. My outlook is certainly looking better. Maybe I won't be bored anymore. Tiberius is a large man with an equally large personality.

As my eyes rove over his features, I realize I don't

consider him my uncle. How could I when I've never known him? My curiosity about him is piqued, and while he seems slightly more approachable than he has been in the past, I decide to ask my questions.

"Are you married?"

His gray eyes shoot to mine. "No." He smirks. "Are you?"

"Considering I'm seventeen, I would have thought the answer to that question was obvious."

"If you ask me personal questions, then expect the same in return." He grins, mirth dancing in his gaze. "What else do you want to know?"

"Why have we never actually met until now?" I sit back in the chair and try to appear relaxed. I certainly feel better than I did before. Maybe I just needed something proper to eat, or what I do not want to admit, company. I'm not sure how I feel about Tiberius. That's a lie. The man with silver eyes causes parts of my body to come alive. Butterflies flutter in my belly. Maybe it's the way he looks at me. I have his sole attention, and I want to keep it.

"There are things that your mother chose to keep from you. I need some time to decide whether or not I tell you what they are."

I watch him, my curiosity stronger than ever. "Would those things change anything?"

He sits forward with his hands on the table. He intertwines his fingers. "The secret Anna and Jude kept would change everything," he says in a deep voice, his eyes blazing. "One day, I may tell you."

I frown. If I'm not mistaken, I catch something within his gaze, as though he is scared to speak of it. I'm more determined than ever to discover what my parents kept from me.

"Not today?"

"Maybe not ever." He stands and tosses his napkin on his plate. "If I do tell you, just remember they are the ones who kept you in the dark." With that, he moves toward the large doorway. He pauses with his hand on the knob and glances over his shoulder. "I will be here from this evening."

"You!" Martha hisses the moment the large front door closes behind Tiberius.

To my horror, my legs tremble at the confrontation I know is seconds away. Martha has always been an evil woman. As soon as Tiberius spoke to her, I knew she would be on me the moment he left. And here she is.

"How dare you complain, you ungrateful little bitch!" Martha charges forward, and I stumble into the wall behind me. She follows and slaps me hard across the face.

Tears fill my eyes as I cradle my throbbing cheek, too stunned to react.

"You think it matters to me that you own this house?" she scoffs. "You know nothing." Her eyes glow with unleashed anger. "I would be careful of who I become friends with, Kinsley," she sneers. "Beckett is—"

I watch her closely as her mouth pulls tight. My heart pounds in my chest while I wonder how to break free of her hold. Martha has never laid a hand on me before, but now the woman before me is finally showing her true colors. I pull myself up to my full five-foot-five height and glare at the woman.

"Do not touch me again," I say, clear and precise. "Next time, I will fight back."

Her eyes narrow. "You are brave all of a sudden." She scowls and looks out of the window. "I may not like you, but if the rumors about Tiberius are true, then I fear for you." Her arm shoots out and holds me against the wall. She is stronger than she appears. "No more whispering into that man's ear about me, or you will be very sorry." With one last shove, she turns and leaves.

I gasp and give into the tears that have been threatening to fall throughout the whole confrontation. My cheek stings as I place it against the cold window and watch the dark clouds roll over the grounds. My stomach is in turmoil. I don't understand what is going on. The one fact that I do know is that I am the ward of Tiberius Beckett. Why him? I have no idea why my father did that. Although I do not trust Martha, her words have me concerned. What does she know about the man to fear for me?

Something else has become apparent. My father knew he was going to die. The changes to his will were completed three weeks before his death. The weight of my new responsibilities as Tiberius's ward settles heavily on my shoulders as I consider the implications of my father's foresight. The realization scares me.

Scared and out of my depth, I turn away from the window. The grandeur of the dining room now seems suffocating, a stark reminder of the impending gloom that arises within me. The portrait of my father hanging on the wall seems to mock me with his knowing gaze, as if he has left behind secrets that I am now forced to uncover. The feeling of unease grows stronger, making me question everything I thought I knew about my family.

Somehow, I manage to pull myself together. I will not let Martha see how much her sharp words and slap across my face have affected me. The woman will not be working at the house for much longer if I have my way. Maybe Tiberius has his own staff that he can bring here. Anyone would be better than the bitter Martha Green.

Chapter Two

I tear off my suit and change into jeans and a tee. After fastening my biker boots, I release a frustrated growl. I don't know what the fuck to do about sweet, innocent Kinsley.

I glare out of my bedroom window, my gaze settling on the house across the lake. I open the door and step out onto the balcony. It's sparsely furnished, with just a table and two chairs, plus a comfortable chaise lounge chair. I've spent many summer nights asleep on it. The outdoors has always called to me, just like the Lake House has.

Memories always swamped me whenever I dropped in on Jude and his family. In recent years, my brother had become uneasy about those visits, which made me wonder what he might have been hiding.

As I rest on the balustrade and gaze out once more across the lake at the house, I wonder what Kinsley is up to. It's something I've wondered for a while now whenever my eyes caught on the house. Thoughts I should never have, even now. At first, it was innocent curiosity about the girl I knew my brother hadn't fathered. But over the past couple of years, I found myself unable to stay away. I've never been introduced to the girl until now. I made sure I always stopped by when I knew she wouldn't be home.

Kinsley grew up rather quickly and became a stunner. I shouldn't be obsessed with her. It's wrong. I know that what I'm feeling would be considered acceptable in the real world, if it weren't for the age difference. I'm not really her uncle. Never have been. Never will be. She doesn't know that yet.

One look at me covered in tattoos would disgust her. My brother never liked ink. Neither had my mother, which is why I have so many.

Kinsley doesn't remember, but when she was told about her parents' deaths, I showed up at the house. She was in shock, so I took charge of her. I held her while she stared into space. I held her some more when her tears finally came. I held her while she slept.

I should have stayed with her so she wasn't alone, but I was dealing with my own grief. Not only that, but I also had to deal with the cops and make arrangements for Jude and Anna. I took my grief and anger and went after the crew who had forced my brother's car off the road. His brakes had been cut, and as the crew chased after them, Jude wasn't able to slow down on the sharp bends of Snake Pass.

I saw the bodies and wish I hadn't. The only bit of luck that evening was that the car hadn't burst into flames.

One crew member was still at large. That was my fault. I lost it with the three my men and I had found. The last one died before he could give me a name. However, I did get one name from the other two. Cannon Edge.

That bastard would pay one day.

I turn my head at the sound of booted feet moving down the hallway outside my bedroom.

"Boss," Salem shouts, knocking on the door. "You in here?"

"Outside," I yell.

He strides out and comes to rest beside me, his gaze following mine. "Do you know what you're doing?"

"I don't have a fucking clue."

He snorts. "I haven't seen you this fucked up before."

I glare at my friend. "I'm not fucked up." My eyes stray back to the Lake House. "Edge is going to come for Kinsley."

"He won't get her. Between you, me, and Jock, we've handpicked all the men who will be around the house. She will be safe."

"Tell the men they don't touch her. Make sure they know she's my family and I will personally kill anyone who causes her harm."

"Yes, boss," Salem drawls, mirth in his voice, which I ignore.

"Prick!"

"Edgar has the weasel in the basement. You wanted to talk to him."

"I want to do more than fucking talk," I snarl.

"Who is he?" I ask Edgar.

The man tied to the chair, with blood and sweat running down his face, is not familiar to me.

"Brinkley," Edgar growls. "I overheard him bragging about knowing where Jubal is hiding out. Why the fuck he'd do that is anyone's guess."

I narrow my gaze and clench my fists. "He's either stupid for flapping his jaws or doesn't know shit, which also makes him stupid."

The man spits blood on the floor. "Fuck you! I know who you are, and you and that bitch will be next."

Before the asshole can blink, I slam my fist into his face. The chair wobbles and then crashes backward.

"Where the fuck is he?"

Although the man laughs, fear sets in. I see it in his eyes and the piss stain on his jeans.

"I lied." He laughs. "I fucking lied. I don't even know who Jubal is."

I crouch beside him as I wipe my hands on a cloth. "You see, I don't believe you. With both mine and

Edge's men looking for Jubal, it would be fucking idiotic to lie about knowing him." I glare at the piece of shit and force myself to stand. To Edgar, I say, "Find out what you can. Then turn him over to Edge."

"No way." Brinkley tugs against his bindings, struggling to break free. "He'll kill me."

Edgar laughs. "Beckett didn't say you have to be alive when I turn you over to Edge."

Pure fear erupts on Brinkley's face.

I walk away. Salem, who had kept to the background, says, "Something doesn't add up with that asshole."

That is what I've been thinking since Edgar brought him in.

Five minutes later, my phone beeps with a message from Edgar. I read it twice before sharing the info with Salem. "Edgar sent the location Brinkley gave him to Prez to get the murdering asshole."

"Fucking hell! Brinkley really was an idiot."

I trust Prez to find Jubal now. All I must do is wait. Something I've been doing since Jude died.

"Make sure the bikes are loaded on to the truck. I don't want to be traveling back and forth between the houses for now."

"They've already been loaded. When do you want to leave?"

"Now."

Salem heads off to round the men up while I stand outside in the fresh air. In truth, I don't want Kinsley in this world of mine, but whether I do or not, it doesn't matter anymore.

Kinsley's life is now tied to mine whether she likes it or not.

Chaptaer Three

I watch as four large black SUVs come up the driveway. My heart thuds in my chest with a mixture of fear and excitement. Tiberius said he would be back.

The moment he steps onto the gravel driveway, his head lifts, and those dark-gray eyes of his land on me. I don't move, and neither does he, until another man says something to him. I shake myself, questioning how the man can ensnare me so easily.

Men in jeans and tees climb from the vehicles. Out of the nine men I count, two are wearing dark suits. Tiberius has changed out of his suit into black jeans and a white tee with sunglasses perched atop his head. It's certainly a different view of the man than the one I previously had. Who are the men with him? They all look dangerous and unapproachable. Surely, they're not all moving into the house.

My head turns as I hear booted feet enter the house. Tiberius gives instructions in a loud voice, and then the footsteps start upstairs. My bedroom door is locked, but that won't keep anyone out who is determined to get inside.

A moment later, there is a knock on my door. "Ms. Kinsley, your, um, uncle, would like you to come downstairs."

I frown at the door. The voice is hesitant, which is not what I expected. Suddenly, more curious than scared, I dash to the door and pull it open. My eyes shoot wide at the huge man standing before me in a lovely dark-gray suit. He is most certainly not what I expected after the voice I heard through the door.

He smirks. "Call me Jock," he says in a calm voice. "You must be Kinsley." He holds out his hand and smiles, but then his eyes narrow as he zeroes in on the side of my face that is red and bruised. "Who did that to you?" His voice deepens.

"The girl is accident prone," Martha says, appearing out of the blue.

The large man stares into my eyes, and I silently

beg him not to say anything because I know that he knows who is responsible. He turns to the woman. "Martha, isn't it? You are wanted in the kitchen." When she hovers, he adds, "Now, woman!"

I wince, which Jock notices. "She won't touch you again. Come. He's waiting for you." I nod, trying to hide my nerves as I follow Jock down the dimly lit hallway. "Don't worry too much about the men in the house. They will leave you alone."

I hesitate at the top of the stairs. "Maybe I should have changed first."

"Nonsense. You look fine." Jock smiles. My eyes travel down my white tee to where my black jeans cling to my skin. Thick socks cover my feet. I didn't bother with my biker boots today.

"Stop fidgeting," Jock says as he shoves me into my father's office—what was my father's office. The heavy door closes behind me. If I didn't know that Tiberius was already in the room, his scent would have given him away.

"You look scared," he comments.

I turn around. "It's unnerving having strange men wandering around my home."

His eyes narrow, and then he is suddenly in front of me. A large, tattooed hand holds my jaw as he turns my face to get a better look at the bruise forming there. I doubt Martha intended on leaving such a sign that she'd hit me.

Tiberius looks into my eyes. "This is because I called her out at lunch." His jaw tightens. "I'll get rid of her."

"No!" I grab hold of his wrist before I snatch my hand back. A sizzle of electricity shoots up my arm. I swallow hard. "I mean." I sigh. "I don't know what I mean."

His fingers gently smooth over the soreness of my cheek before he steps back. "That woman—"

"Boss," a dark-skinned man interrupts us. He grins when he sees me, and I don't think I've ever seen anyone with such perfect, white teeth before.

My lips twist into a smile when I realize the man is really being friendly. "Hello," I offer.

Tiberius narrows his eyes between the two of us and snaps, "Saul! I do not pay you to drool over my"— he clears his throat—"niece."

"No, sir!" Saul snaps his focus to Tiberius, who hasn't stopped glaring. "I came to tell you the truck is five minutes out."

"Okay. Get them moving once they arrive."

Saul nods and exits the room without another glance my way.

"Are the men moving in as well?" I ask the silently brooding man. I ignore the fact we're dressed similarly.

"Yes." He enters my space, and it takes all my will power not to back down. "You will not encourage them."

It takes me a moment to understand what he is saying. When I do, my eyes widen in surprise. "He's far too old for me." I don't add that my taste in men centers on the man in front of me.

"So dramatic." He steps back and looks irritated. "Regardless, do not speak to my men."

The sound of a loud vehicle approaching breaks the silence as the wheels crunch on the driveway.

I look out the window and frown at the eighteen-wheeler. "What is in there?"

"Furniture, among other things." He pauses in the doorway. "Do you want any of the furniture from your parents' bedroom before I have it destroyed?"

"No, thank you." That is something I do not want. "However, if you wish to get rid of my father's desk, I would like that."

He nods. "Dinner will be in an hour or so."

"Why don't you step away from the window?" Jock suggests.

"I'm curious. I've seen Tiberius every now and again over the years; however, I never actually met him until the reading of the will. I mean, he was at the funeral, but we didn't speak. My father thought he was doing the right thing by making me his ward. So, I must trust in that." It doesn't stop me from admiring the fit of his jeans and tee as he moves.

"Your father knew Beckett would protect you if he asked. You will be safe here."

I turn to Jock and frown. "You call him by his family name?"

"Habit." Jock smiles. "How about a warm drink in the kitchen. I could do with a cup of coffee myself."

"Okay." I follow beside him and come to a stop. "What are they carrying upstairs?"

"A bed."

"He doesn't want to sleep in my parents' bed, so he brought his own." I glance at Jock for confirmation.

He nods.

"I suppose that makes sense." I sigh. "There are a

lot of things that do not make sense to me, though. Many in fact, and I don't know where to start."

"Let's have that cup of coffee," he suggests and leads me toward the kitchen. "Problem?" he asks when I come to a sudden stop before stepping foot inside.

"I've never been allowed inside the kitchen," I whisper.

"From what I have been told, this is your house, which means this is your kitchen." He smirks and pushes his way inside. A growl comes out of his mouth when he sees Martha at the far end of the room. "You lay a hand on this girl again, and I will show you how hard a man as big as me can hit."

Oh God.

"You took the words right out of my mouth, Jock." Tiberius moves into the room. "This is your last chance, Ms. Green." His steely eyes narrow on the woman before he shoots a look I can't decipher at Jock. "Do not bring my niece over to the dark side while I'm in the office."

"Wouldn't dream of it."

Tiberius snorts and turns his attention to me. His eyes linger as he grabs an apple on his way out of the room.

Jock claps his hands. "Show's over. Now, can someone show us where we can make our coffee?"

"It's behind you. Nothing too fancy," a timid voice replies.

I turn to find a former employee. The young woman is maybe three years older than me. She's also the daughter of one of Martha's friends, and I'm sure she fears the vile woman too. "Thank you, Marie." I smile at her. "I didn't know you were working here again."

"Mr. Beckett called the old staff back." Marie moves closer. "I am sorry about your parents, Kinsley." She grabs my hand and squeezes.

"Thank you," I say, choking on the words.

I turn my attention to Jock, who's pouring two cups of coffee. He passes me a cup, then places a hand to my back and guides me back out along the hallway.

"The girl seemed nice," he says when we reach the living room.

"Marie is." I sit at one end of the sofa and inhale the rich aroma before I take a sip. "This is very good."

"I made it, so of course it is." He chuckles. "No one comes between me and my coffee."

"Did Tiberius ask you to be nice to me?"

His eyes dance. "He told me not to let you out of my sight."

"Hmm," I mutter.

I sit back and listen to the men putting the bed together upstairs. Hammering comes from the office, which I ignore. I don't want to know what other changes are taking place. Instead, I wonder about Jock. I sense the man was truly angry when he discovered I was hit. He will follow Tiberius's orders in the end, which means I can't trust him as much as I want to. It would be nice to not be so alone anymore.

I guess I will be safe from the outside world in the house. But will I be safe from Tiberius?

Available Now!

OTHER BOOKS BY AUTHOR

Hawke's Ridge

Maddox · Colton (2026)

Den Hollows

One of Six · Two of Six (2026)

Den of Filth (New MC Series 2025)

Reckless Wilder (2026)

Fifth Realm Series (Romantasy)

Quiver of Chaos · Wings & Arrows (2026)

Standalone Romantasy

Persephone Unchained

Tallulah James Mystery

Dead and a Murder or Two · Dead and the Wedding Crashers · Dead and a Deadly Deed · Dead and a Best Friend

Boston Bay Vikings

Camden · Bennett · Ethan · Sutton · Carter · Bryson · Ivan · Theo · Noah · Knox · Jericho · Roman

Boston Bay Vikings Minor League

Lake · Rhodes · Nikoli · Dario · Madden · Bradford

Single Titles

Butterflies and Darkness · Come Back to Me · Indecent Villain · Lawful · Love Stryker · Tears in the Rain · Whispers of Yesterday

Holiday Season

Holiday Kisses in the Snow · Jingle Bells

Romantic Suspense Series

Twenty Eight Days · The Next Victim (2025)

Blossom Creek

Christmas at Emelia's · A Rake in Blossom Creek · Heatwave in Blossom Creek · Secret Love in Blossom Creek · Mischief in Blossom Creek · Runaway Bride in Blossom Creek · Naughty & Nice in Blossom Creek

Bad Boy Rockers

My Brother's Girl · Past Sins · My Best Friend's Sister · Never Let Go · Saving Jace · Silent Night (Novella)

Kincaid Sisters

Meant to be Mine · You Were Always Mine · Will You be Mine

McKenzie Brothers

Playing with the Boss · A McKenzie Wedding (Novella) · Playing with Fire · Playing with Desire · Playing with Trouble · Playing with their Hearts · A McKenzie Christmas (Novella)

De La Fuente Family (McKenzie Spinoff)

Love in Montana · Love in Purgatory · Love in Bloom · Love in Country · Love in Flame · Love in Game · Love in Education

McKenzie Cousins

(McKenzie Spinoff)

Baby Makes Three · A Business Decision · Secret Kisses · Kissing Cousins · If Only · Princess & the Puck · A Bakers Delight · A Cowboy for Christmas · A Secret Affair · One Christmas · The Pregnant Professor · It Started with a Kiss

Novella's

Educate Me · One Dance · Pure

ABOUT THE AUTHOR

While Lexi is the author of the chick lit series, Tallulah James Mystery, and the fantasy/romance series, The Fifth Realm, she is also the author of over seventy novels. Based in Ireland, this British author has been writing since 2013.

Follow on social media:

Website: http://lexibuchanan.net
Email: authorlexibuchanan@gmail.com

facebook.com/lexibuchananauthor
x.com/AuthorLexi
instagram.com/authorlexib
bookbub.com/author/lexi-buchanan
amazon.com/Lexi-Buchanan/e/B009SPA94U